WANTED: OUTBACK WIFE

BARBARA MCMAHON

Prologue

The email arrived just before bed. Rennie had been expecting it and took a deep breath before clicking it open.

Dear Miss Davidson,

My aunt's attorney has undoubtedly filled you in on the reason for this letter. He has assured me that the best solution to the problems facing us would be to marry. I had no prior knowledge of the terms of my great-aunt Marjorie's will, but her attorney has made it clear that its conditions are entirely legal. The restrictions that the inheritance comes jointly to us only in the event that we marry each other within a year were shocking to say the least. Knowing how I feel about matrimony, I'm even more astounded at my aunt's restrictions than you must be. Her attorney has suggested that if we choose to fulfill the terms of the will we view a marriage between us as strictly a business arrangement. He urges us to take the necessary steps to settle the matter.

I know he has discussed the situation with you. In hopes that you are amiable to the suggestion, I am writing to inquire if that is the case. To make sure my aunt's attorney has not misled you, I must tell you Silver Creek Station is in Australia's outback. We have a successful cattle operation with many amenities. However, the nearest town is over an hour's drive distance. My aunt mentioned her dear friend, your grandmother, many times in her letters. She told us how the ranches in the arid part of Texas were similar to the stations around here so you should have an idea of what it's like here.

My brother and his wife died six months ago. I have had the care of their child, Kerry, since then. She's not yet two. Her grandparents are now demanding custody of her. I want the child raised here at the station and am willing to do whatever I need to in order to make sure she has a happy home. While the thought of inheriting half of Aunt Marjorie's estate is appealing, more importantly I want a mother for Kerry.

Love is not a requirement in an arrangement such as this, but I will insist on loving kindness for Kerry. She is in dire need of a woman's influence. In exchange for your loyalty to my family, I will provide a home for you all your life.

Your share of the inheritance is, of course, yours to spend as you like. I believe the money would help with your grandmother's care.

If you are interested in pursuing this odd arrangement, please let me know. As you probably can gather, time is of the essence. If I hear in the affirmative, I will make the necessary arrangements.

Yours, Hunter Bradshaw

There it was, laid out plain as day. Now the final choice was up to her.

1

I'm not ready, Rennie Davidson thought in panic, butterflies tripping in her stomach. Stepping from the small twin-engine plane into the shimmering heat of the Australian day, she gazed unseeingly at the empty land surrounding the small airport. Beyond was the small town. She licked her lips, feeling the heavy pounding of her heart. What was she doing here in Boolong Creek, Northern Territory? Was she out of her mind? It wasn't too late for second thoughts, was it?

Smoothing her shoulder-length honey-blond hair back from her heated face, her blue eyes wide and glazed, she was slightly surprised to find that her fingers were trembling. She quickly balled her hands into fists. Taking a deep breath, she looked around once more as if the barren landscape could offer an escape.

She didn't have to go through with it.

She blinked. Really, what choice did she have? Nothing had changed. Of course she had to go through with it. It was business, pure and simple. And she desperately needed the money for her grandmother.

Seeking some relief from the sun's rays, she walked around the side of the solitary terminal, hugging the shade. Stepping around a man leaning insolently against the drab terminal without giving him a glance, her thoughts a thousand miles away, she wondered when she'd be picked up. How much longer did she have to get her nervousness under control?

"Rennie Davidson?" a firm voice asked behind her right shoulder.

She swung around.

The tall, well-built man leaned casually against the weathered wood of the small airport building, studying her from beneath the wide brim of his hat. She took in his broad shoulders, his strong brown neck rising from the open throat of the blue shirt he wore.

Fascinated by the sight before her, she let her eyes drift down his body. Muscular brown arms were crossed casually over his chest, his shirt-sleeves rolled up. His hips were narrow, his legs powerful in faded jeans, one bent as he rested his foot against the weathered boards of the small building. Dusty leather boots encased his feet.

She brought her gaze up to clash with his and she could feel herself grow almost giddy.

"Yes," she replied, moving to stand warily before him. "I'm Rennie Davidson."

She was suddenly glad she was wearing her trim navy blue pants with a crisp, frilly white blouse that added a touch of femininity, glad she'd brushed her hair before leaving the plane. For a moment she wanted to impress the man in front of her.

"I'm Hunter Bradshaw," he said lazily. "I wasn't sure you'd come."

Rennie looked into his clear gray eyes. His dark skin looked like seasoned teak, bronzed by the hot Australian sun, weathered by the winds. His light eyes were startling with his tanned face and dark hair, but it was a combination she immediately found fascinating. His voice was deep and strong and wonderful with his Australian accent.

Rennie wondered briefly if she'd missed something. She shook her head to clear it, to see if she had matters confused. This was Hunter Bradshaw? This self-assured, confident male who stood before her positively radiating strength and sexuality? Tall, dominant, commanding, he was nothing at all what she'd envisioned. How could he not have already been married?

His great-aunt had been right on the good-looking part, she thought, clutching at sanity. He was gorgeous.

"I said I'd come," she replied as her thoughts spun into a hundred different directions.

He offered his hand. Rennie hesitated only a moment before taking his firm grasp. His fingers were hard and calloused, warm and firm. She felt a shock of awareness course through her at his touch, every nerve-ending quivering, her heart racing. Stepping back nervously, she almost yanked her hand free, clenching her fingers into a fist, her breathing curiously unsteady.

She wanted to step away, escape the magnetism of his eyes, the pull of attraction she unexpectedly experienced. Even with Stuart she'd never been so aware of herself as a woman, so aware of the sheer maleness of a man. She couldn't possibly marry him; he'd overwhelm her in an hour!

Hunter Bradshaw topped her by several inches. While she was tall, he had to be well over six feet. The width of his muscular shoulders did nothing to minimize his stature. His bush hat was pulled low on his face, shading it from the sun, but she saw his eyes study her and the heat within her continued to build—a strange intoxicating heat that made her so very glad she was a woman.

"You're not what I expected," he said as his glance skimmed across her cheeks, touched on her lips and moved down to scan her body.

Without any indication of what he was thinking, he pushed away from the wall and started toward the plane, his gait loose and smooth. Assured, as if he owned the whole territory.

"We'll collect your luggage and then have some lunch. We still have another hour's drive to the homestead," he said.

As he began walking he yanked his dusty hat lower.

Rennie turned to fall into step, wishing she had sunglasses to shelter her eyes from the strong glare of the noontime sun, to offer her some measure of protection from the penetrating gaze of the man beside her. Promising herself she'd pick up a pair as soon as possible, she hurried to keep up with his longer stride.

"What had you expected?" she asked.

Was he disappointed? Did he want to call off the arrangement? Was he changing his mind or still determined to continue with their plan?

Her own doubts returned. Were they foolish to make a marriage of convenience in this day and age? Who would expect her to carry through with it?

Yet, perversely, she didn't want him to change his mind.

He shrugged, reaching the plane, lifting her cases from the ground where the pilot had placed them.

"I didn't expect you to be so pretty for one thing," he said, frowning.

That caught her by surprise. He didn't appear to notice she was as tongue-tied as a teenager as he led her to a rusty, battered, dusty utility truck. Was it a compliment? He didn't appear to like the fact.

He noticed her hesitation as he nodded toward the vehicle.

"Bloody impossible to keep anything clean when the dust rises. I use this around the station, on and off road, so it looks the worse for it. But the inside's clean."

She nodded, watching as he easily tossed her heavy suitcases into the back, wondering if he was now asking himself why he'd agreed to send across the world for a woman he'd never met.

From what she could see, Rennie thought Hunter Bradshaw would have no difficulty in getting a wife. It was more likely he'd have trouble keeping the women away.

His looks were dynamic, his manner assured and assertive. Perhaps, having met her, he'd changed his mind.

Illogically, in light of her recent doubts, Rennie fervently hoped this was not the case. And her promised share of the inheritance had nothing to do with it.

Hunter helped her into the cab. She was glad for the protection of the cotton trousers—she could burn her legs on the scorching vinyl seat. When he climbed in he turned slightly in his seat to study her. Rennie returned his regard gravely, unwilling to let him know how her heart raced or of the heat that raged through her.

"There's a nice little place here in town that serves lunch;

we'll eat and discuss things before heading for the station."

"That sounds fine—Hunter."

She was pleased with the way she had said his name, so casually. Pleased that her voice hadn't cracked with the tension that was so tight she was afraid she'd shatter. Perhaps he wouldn't guess how awkward she felt, how suddenly unsure of herself and the entire situation she'd become.

His lips tilted in a half-smile as he put the car in gear. He'd guessed.

Eagerly she looked around the town as they drove through, interested in all she saw. There was one main street, paved, but with dust so thick it looked like a dirt road. Several businesses and shops lined the street, though few people were on the sidewalks. A two-storied department store dominated an entire block. She glimpsed some houses down the side-streets, their gardens offering a bright spot of color. All in all Boolong Creek was a small place.

And she didn't see water anywhere. Where was the creek?

Hunter pulled up before a small place called Mattie's. Upon entering, Rennie recognized how popular it was. The pub was almost full, only one or two tables were vacant. Hunter led the way to one in the back which would afford them some degree of privacy. He nodded and spoke to several people in passing but didn't stop to talk at length to anyone or introduce her.

Rennie scanned the room when they sat, her blond hair falling a little over her cheeks, sheltering her from Hunter's penetrating gaze. Acutely aware of him as she had never been so aware of another, she wanted to give herself some breathing space—needed it.

A waitress came to take their orders, chatting easily with Hunter. Again he didn't introduce her and Rennie's belief that he'd changed his mind was strengthened. If no one knew her, or why she'd come, there'd be less talk when she left. She looked up as Hunter ordered, wondering what he'd told people here. Did everyone know he'd sent to America for an unknown bride?

"Give us meat pies, chips and something cold to drink."

He didn't ask Rennie what she wanted, confidently ordering for both of them.

She flashed him a sharp look, wondering if he was always so sure of himself and others. If that was the case, how could he agree to an arranged marriage, even as a business arrangement? He didn't have the look of a man that could be made to do anything he didn't want.

The waitress returned quickly with their plates. Rennie was grateful. She found the silence growing between them daunting. But she was determined not to be the one to break it.

When the first pangs of hunger were satisfied, Hunter broke the silence.

"Your trip was all right?"

She glanced up, awareness shimmering through her at his proximity. The table wasn't much protection from his potent attraction. She wasn't used to reacting so strongly to a man. Taking a deep breath, she tried to gain a measure of control. She'd opted for this solution and she'd see it through if it killed her.

"Yes, thank you. Thank you for sending me the ticket."

Glad to hear that her voice was strong, she sat back in her

chair and regarded him thoughtfully.

He nodded, his eyes narrowed as he stared at her.

"The situation's awkward, isn't it?" he asked forthrightly.

Color stained her cheeks, but she didn't pretend to misunderstand him.

"Yes...I'm not sure—"

He interrupted, not unkindly, "I'm not all that sure myself, now that the reality is here. I thought Americans were an independent lot. Yet you're here ready to marry a man you just met."

Looking around the room, stalling for time, Rennie wondered how to respond. She hadn't expected such a forthright attitude. Somehow she'd hoped he'd gloss over things a little. Finally she looked back and met his gaze, then picked up a chip and studied it, as if unsure what to say next.

"I need the money I'll get by marrying you. And the thought of being a mother to a little girl who needs one is very appealing. I realized that there could be worse things."

"Ah, so I'm a bit above the fate worse than death?"

"I—um—want to be needed."

She hadn't meant to insult him.

"And Kerry and I need you." He nodded as if he understood. "So it's not entirely the money?" Skepticism laced his tone.

"No, though in all honesty the thought of turning that amount down would give anyone second thoughts."

She grinned nervously, a dimple touching the soft skin of her cheek. Then she grew serious again.

"The money is essential if I'm to obtain the medical care my grandmother needs. I believe I wrote you she is quite ill."

"That explains why the urgency for the money. How did she feel about you coming here?"

"Excited for me," Rennie replied thoughtfully. "She and your aunt Marjorie were such close friends for so long, she feels she knows you. And she likes the idea of me mothering the baby. I'm to send pictures."

She already missed her grandmother. She'd been the only stability in a lifetime of being shunted from place to place.

"I think I ought to make sure you understand the situation," he continued, leaning back in his chair, watching her closely.

His silvery eyes seemed to touch her very soul.

"My grandfather lives with me at the homestead. When Alex and Tessa died, little Kerry came to live with us. Her other relatives, Tessa's parents, are now fighting for custody. Alex named me as guardian, and I want to raise his daughter. But the child needs a mother. The courts want a stable home for her. If I can't provide it, they'll award custody to Tessa's parents."

She nodded. There was more to Hunter's wanting to marry than just the money, as well. A child's future was at stake. It made the idea of a marriage between them seem less cold-blooded, less mercenary.

He paused a moment, glanced around the restaurant, then back, obviously making up his mind to continue.

"But I'm not looking for a short-term solution. If you're planning to marry, get your money and then skip, forget it. I want someone for Kerry at least until she's grown. I'm looking for permanence."

Rennie nodded, her eyes wide. She hadn't thought much

beyond getting married. Of course he'd want the stability of a long-term relationship for the little girl. And Rennie wouldn't want to subject little Kerry to the kind of disruptions she'd experienced in her life.

She was committed, for the next twenty years, at least. She took a breath. It was almost overwhelming. Had there been another solution, she'd have chosen it in a heartbeat.

"I didn't agree to come here for a few days, to get married and leave. I've arranged to have everything I own shipped here. My suitcases are only part of my things. I'm not here for a short time," she said firmly, a determined light in her blue eyes.

She'd ransomed her future for the chance to help her grandmother. But she'd abide by her decision.

He studied her for a long moment, his eyes impaling hers.

"I never planned to marry once Alex married Tessa. I thought they'd see to the future generation, have plenty of sons. But that changed with the car crash. Kerry needs a woman, a mother. For her sake, I'll provide a mother."

"And for the money," she added.

"That's part of it, of course. But I also want to maintain Silver Creek Station. There's work to be done and it's costly," he replied.

Rennie nodded. She'd known this before she came. Not about his grandfather living with them, but the rest.

"I'll do my best to be a good mother."

"You ought to know up front I don't believe in love. It's a fantasy for starry-eyed women and insipid poets, so don't plan on flowers and candy," Hunter continued, his eyes steady as he looked into hers. "I don't feel it fair to marry someone who might come to care for me more than I would for them. Imagine herself in love with me. Or expect wildly romantic evenings. Ours would be strictly a business arrangement."

She nodded again.

"Do you know why your aunt would make such a will?" she asked.

She was still puzzled by the terms that had left Marjorie's vast fortune to herself and this man only if they married each other.

"Aunt Marjorie was always trying her hand at matchmaking. Even from Texas. You came highly recommended." He smiled mockingly. "I understand you like a quiet life, know something about cattle from working as an accountant for the cattleman's association in Texas, aren't into wild extravagances, and you're a good cook, and housekeeper."

He stopped, a scowl growing as he became aware of Rennie's expression.

She glared at him.

"I didn't get a recommendation for you. Maybe you'd like to register your good points before we go any farther."

He made it sound as if he had picked her out of a catalog.

"Look, let's get one thing clear. Neither of us would be marrying if it weren't for my aunt Marjorie's inheritance, right? So far this arrangement brings us both something we want. You get the money to help with your grandmother, I get a mother for Kerry. As long as we keep that in mind, we'll brush along and everything will work out."

"It sounds to me as if you want more than brushing along with this arrangement, talking about permanence," she snapped in reply.

He leaned over the table and grabbed her wrist, his fingers hot and hard against her delicate skin.

"My family isn't noted for its long-lived marriages. My grandmother died young, my mother deserted my father when Alex was just a baby, and Tessa left Alex just before they were killed. I plan to break the trend. I expect this marriage to endure until one or the other of us dies of old age. Is that clear?"

"Perfectly."

A *frisson* of anxiousness swept through her. She hoped she could stay. What if she was as unstable in relationships as her mother?

"I'll give you no cause to end it. Can you say the same?" she said more bravely than she felt.

His grip loosened and slowly he traced his thumb across the fine veins exposed in her pale skin.

"I'll give no reason to end it."

She looked down at his hand, shivering slightly at the response that raced through her. Her pulse sped up, her blood heated as if his hand were a candle. He had big hands, tanned, strong, hardworking; she'd felt the calluses against her fingers earlier, could now feel the slight abrasion of his thumb against her own smooth skin. It was easier to study his hands than look at his face, meet his gaze. He was strong and sturdy and overwhelmingly masculine.

She'd be his wife, yet not have to worry about him falling in love. He'd been clear on that. She licked her lips, not finding the thought as distasteful as she'd thought she would. As she flicked him a glance an appalling thought flashed through her mind. Did she have to worry about herself falling in love with him?

"I came all the way from Texas so I guess that's as good a commitment to this business arrangement as any," she said, her voice sweet and soft compared to his Australian twang.

She wanted to make sure he knew she was planning on holding to the *business* aspect of their situation. Her heart sped up again at the mere thought of marriage and she tugged her hand away, lest he feel her increased pulse-rate.

"Fine. I've made arrangements for the wedding. We can be married this afternoon."

Were butterflies going to be permanent residents in her stomach? she wondered. They'd flared again at Hunter's words.

True, she'd committed to marry him, so there was no reason to delay, but she had thought somehow that she'd have a few days to get to know him first.

Yet what would that accomplish? She really didn't want to get married at all, but the unexpected chance to help Gram was too important to miss. Still, she'd never expected to be married as soon as she got off the plane. He was talking about being married in a few minutes!

"Any problem?" he asked, raising an eyebrow, as if attuned to her sudden uncertainty, her reluctance. Could he read her mind?

She shook her head, taking another chip and dipping it into the ketchup, hoping desperately that she looked calm and confident.

"No problem. I'm surprised you wanted to get married today. You received all the paperwork I sent?" Copes of the formal documents were in her purse.

He nodded. "It's a long drive to the station. I've already

taken off most of today. I don't want to have to come back into town for a while," he explained, his gray eyes studying her, his gaze roaming over her face, her shoulders, touching the swell of her breasts.

Rennie wished he wouldn't stare at her. She felt vulnerable beneath his penetrating gaze. And she didn't like her own reaction every time he looked at her. The glimmer in his silvery eyes evoked sensations that threatened her precarious balance.

"A good practical reason for getting married today," she agreed, thrusting away the small pang of disappointment that he couldn't even take time from the station another day to come in for a wedding. His own wedding.

She glanced down at her travel-worn outfit, and then across at his work clothes. Somehow she'd expected a bit more formality at her wedding. She thought of the white dress she'd bought. Should she mention it? Probably not. He'd think she was trying to romanticize the situation and she already knew he was scornful of such ideas.

"I have a car at home you can use. You won't be tied to the homestead, Rennie, if that's worrying you. But I don't have time to be traveling back and forth here, or into Sydney or Darwin for nightlife. I run the station. I can't be away for long."

"I didn't expect night life. I'll pull my weight in this arrangement, you don't need to worry about that. You were clear in your emails about what to expect. Anyway I'm not used to bright lights and nightclubs."

The only times she'd reveled in a glamorous night life had been with Stuart. She now equated that lifestyle with men like him, men she wanted to avoid.

"You won't get it here. Tessa used to nag Alex incessantly to move to Sydney, complaining that Silver Creek Station was the back of beyond and boring."

"You mustn't find it so," she said.

Was he comparing her to Tessa?

"No, but Tessa came from Sydney and felt that the excitement of the big city was infinitely preferable to the routine of a cattle station in the outback. Any other questions before we go?"

Hunter had finished eating and picked up his hat.

Rennie had a thousand questions, but none that couldn't be answered over time. None that had to be answered before they married.

Married!

She took a deep breath, the meat pie sitting like a rock in her stomach. She'd been committed since she left Texas. There was no holding back now.

"No other questions. I'm ready."

An hour later Rennie sat beside her new husband as he drove east on the two-lane sealed road. The ceremony had been brief and brisk. She glanced at the shiny golden ring on her finger, surprised that he'd bought her one, and even more surprised that it fit. How could he have known her ring size?

The ceremony had been unlike the lavish wedding she and Stuart had planned, but suitable enough for the business arrangement that was between her and Hunter. Though she hadn't expected to be married so casually and so hurriedly, she'd none the less made her vows with all sincerity, determined to make him a good wife.

She'd show him she could be depended upon. She felt a

bit like a bought bride, but knowing her grandmother would be given the finest care made it all worthwhile.

She should be counting her blessings that the opportunity had even arisen. The money that would come to her upon this marriage would assure her grandmother the best care possible. There was every chance of a complete recovery.

Rennie owed that to her grandmother and was happy to be able to repay her in some small way for all the older woman had done for her.

Her eyes drifted from the ring to study the man beside her. Her husband. He looked the same as when she'd first met him a couple of hours ago, confident, at ease. Not as if his world had suddenly tilted on its axis, which was how Rennie felt.

Of course for Hunter it hadn't. His life would go on much as it had before. Only now he had someone to take care of Kerry, keep his house and leave him free to devote himself to running the station.

Only her world had tilted. Everything was different. Taking in his long legs, the strong hands that held the wheel, the firm line of his jaw, Rennie wondered again if she'd made the right decision. She'd forsaken all she knew to start a new life in Australia with a stranger.

She shivered slightly, intrigued by the strong pull of attraction that she felt around him. He was unlike any of the men she'd known in Texas. Could she cope, hold her own? Or would she come to regret this day?

2

Rennie could almost touch the shimmering tension between them, an arc sparking in the hot air. Never had she been so physically conscious of another person.

Tearing her eyes away, she stared out the window at the open. Only time would tell if their arrangement would endure, but she'd do all in her power to uphold her end of the bargain. And giving into flights of fantasy wasn't part of the arrangement.

As she stared unseeingly over the flat landscape she replayed in her mind the instant when the minister had told Hunter to kiss his bride. His gray eyes had burned into hers. Her cheek had almost blazed from the light touch of his lips. She'd felt the sensation jolt through her. She hadn't expected anything like that reaction.

What would it have been like for him to kiss her full on the mouth? Have him press her body against his and kiss her as if they were lovers?

She tried to turn her thoughts away from such speculation. It wasn't likely to happen soon, if ever. Which was what she had expected. It was the way she wanted it, wasn't it?

"How different is this from Texas?"

Startled to hear him speak after being silent for so long, she swung her eyes to him. "Pardon?"

"I asked how different is this landscape from Texas."

He spoke slowly, as if to someone who didn't understand English.

She began to pay attention to the silvery green scrub brush, the occasional acacia trees that dotted the land. The grasses were dried, cropped and dusty.

Smiling, she replied, "I almost feel at home. West Texas is also rather barren and desolate. I don't recognize the trees, but the scrub brush looks similar to the sage of home, and dried grass looks the same the world over. We have tumble weeds, though."

"Think you'll feel at home, then?" he asked.

"It's similar. I should settle fine. I won't be looking to move to a city, in any event."

That was what he was really asking, wasn't it?

"This denotes the boundary of Silver Creek Station," Hunter said as they drove past a rock pillar dividing endless miles of barbed-wire fence.

"How large is it?" she asked politely.

The land looked the same as that surrounding the town though she could see some low hills in the distance. How could anyone tell where one property ended and another began?

"We have about a hundred thousand square kilometers," he said casually.

She turned to him, astonished.

"A hundred thousand square kilometers? Good grief, that's huge!"

She tried to relate that to acres and compare it to the ranches she knew in Texas. It was mind-boggling.

"It's too dry to support the same amount of cattle per acre as the stations in New South Wales, so we need a lot more land to run a herd of any size."

"Is it all as dry as this?"

"In the dry it is. We have artesian wells located around the property to provide water during the long dry season. In the wet we get rain, have spreader dams to catch and hold as much as possible."

"How many men on the ranch—I mean station?"

"At the homestead there's me and my grandfather plus about a dozen stock men. Four of them have families. We have two smaller places south of here that managers oversee. My grandfather doesn't do much now but try to boss everyone from the house. He turned over the day-to-day running of the operation to me a couple of years ago. Wanted early retirement, he said."

Hunter shook his head.

"He just wanted an excuse to be able to tinker with his machines and not worry about the cattle."

"And your parents?"

His face was impassive as he flicked her a quick glance.

"Haven't seen my mother since she walked out on us thirty years ago. My father lives in Sydney, works in shipping."

"Will I be cooking for everyone at the station?"

She changed the subject fast, feeling the intensity beneath Hunter's control at his last answer.

Suddenly the reality of how little she knew about the set-up hit her. The thought of cooking for sixteen or more people every day was almost overpowering.

"No, our family eats together. The single men have their

own cook and stay in the compound not too far from our house."

"Who's been watching Kerry since her parents died?"

"Grandfather and one of the stock men's wives, Maggie Taylor. But Kerry's been here for a while and is a real handful. Plus Maggie has her own household."

He glanced over at her, again running his eyes over her in the way that made Rennie forget her resolve to keep her distance from her new husband and made her long to inch closer. She swallowed.

She'd never considered herself particularly attractive, but with Hunter she felt positively alluring and very feminine. Did he look at all women that way?

"Know much about kids?" Hunter asked.

She shook her head.

"But I can learn and I have some books about childcare on my Kindle."

Could she really cope with an eighteen-month-old? She'd never been around children, though she'd yearned to be a mother, to give her children a happier childhood than she'd had.

He swore softly beneath his breath and turned back to the road.

"I thought women knew all about being mothers."

"Not without having babies. And I haven't had much opportunity for that," she said scathingly. "Don't worry, I'll learn fast."

"I hope so. That's the main reason I married you."

"I thought it was for your aunt's money," she said sweetly, seething with anger at his tone and the fresh reminder that this marriage wasn't something either of them especially wanted.

She at least was making an effort—couldn't he?

"The money will be helpful. My primary reason is Kerry."

"And that's one of my reasons, too."

"Though you need the money."

"I do, but my grandmother won't live forever, even if she can beat this illness. Whereas you and I will be married forever even when the immediate need for the money passes. You needn't worry. I'll be a good mother to Kerry."

Kerry was likely to be the only good thing to come of the marriage, and Rennie refused to jeopardize that. She needed something good to come from it all.

He turned off the main road onto the long, narrow driveway that led to the homestead and Rennie's stomach betrayed her nervousness again. Fatigue battled with apprehension and she longed for some privacy. Too much was happening too fast. It'd probably be night before she'd have any time to herself, though.

In only moments she'd be meeting the rest of Hunter's family, and be plunged into her role as Hunter's wife. She swallowed hard, trying to still her nerves. She was Hunter's wife—she'd better get used to it!

When she spotted the house, she studied it avidly as they drew closer.

"The house is bigger than I expected. Do you rattle around in it, just the three of you?" she asked.

"It's an old homestead, built for a large family. My great-grandfather built it. Though they never had any children but my grandfather. He had one son; my dad had two. We're used to the space. A few of the rooms don't even have furniture in them."

Two stories tall, a wide veranda running across the front, it had once been white, but the red dust had prevailed and now it blended in with the dirt upon which it sat. A row of mature gum trees gave some shade and broke any wind from the west, their silvery green leaves fluttering in the late afternoon breeze.

"And the other buildings?"

Beyond the house several buildings stretched out almost like a small village; a large gray barn was close by.

"Some are housing for the stock men. There's the horse barn, the holding pens for the cattle, a couple of sheds that house machinery. Thought you knew ranching."

"I worked for a cattleman's association, but I lived in town. It's in the heart of ranching country, but I never lived on a ranch," she explained.

When he drew to a stop near the back door, Hunter turned to her.

"Welcome to Silver Creek Station, Mrs. Bradshaw. Let's both hope this works."

Mrs. Bradshaw.

She smiled and looked away, the smile fading as she faced her new home. Even the potent attraction she felt in Hunter's proximity faded as the magnitude of what she'd done finally hit her. She hadn't vacillated after her decision had been made in Texas. She'd deliberated on her choices, considered all angles.

Marjorie's will had been most unexpected, but clear–half her considerable estate to Rennie in the event that she married her nephew within the year.

And she'd needed the money so desperately for Gram.

She'd committed herself, burnt her bridges. It was up to her to make it work. Like Hunter she hoped it would for both their sakes.

"Come on, they'll be inside," he said gently as if he suspected her trepidation.

His understanding was unexpected. And welcomed.

Hunter led the way in through the kitchen. Rennie was pleasantly surprised to see that it was spotless. Somehow she'd expected a male-only household to be cluttered. This was clean and tidy, and as plain as the day it was built. There were no rugs, no curtains, no place mats on the scrubbed table to break the drabness.

"About time you got home. Was Ben's plane late?"

A big man in his late sixties stepped into the kitchen. When he caught sight of Rennie, he frowned, running his eyes over her in appraisal, his dark gaze thoughtful. In his arms was a dirty little ragamuffin of a child.

Rennie's eyes were drawn immediately to Kerry. Her heart dropped. This was not the picture-perfect baby she'd been expecting. The little girl's brown hair had been hacked off until it was as short as a boy's. She wore a dusty T-shirt and diapers. Brown legs and dirty feet dangled as she stared at Rennie with large brown eyes. She clung to the old man like a lifeline.

"Grandpa, this is Rennie. She and I got married this afternoon. That's why we're late getting here," Hunter said, his tone neutral, but his eyes narrowed as if waiting for a reaction that was not long in coming.

Shaking his head, the old man ran his eyes down Rennie then turned to Hunter.

"You're a fool, boy. This one'll never stay—too feminine and frivolous for this kind of place. Be gone in less than a month. Don't know why you wanted a damned bloody Yank anyway. Bloody foolishness the whole thing, if you ask me."

"Grandpa." Hunter's voice had a warning edge to it.

Rennie instinctively moved nearer her husband. His strength was almost palpable, the kind she could rely on.

"We've been through all this before. Rennie is my wife now and you remember that!"

"Be gone before the month," the older man grumbled.

He was as tall as his grandson, but heavier. Displaying some of the strength of character that Hunter had demonstrated, he appeared a formidable man.

"She's not going anywhere," Hunter said, his feet braced, his voice firm and clear in the silence.

His gaze was calm as it clashed with his grandfather's.

"Bloody hell!"

He hesitated a long moment, meeting Hunter's stare, then backed down and turned to Rennie.

"Welcome to Silver Creek Station, *Mrs. Bradshaw*," he said grudgingly. Shifting the little girl, the older man offered his hand. "I'm George Bradshaw, Hunter's grandfather. You can call me Grandpa too, if you've a mind to. Might as well for as long as you're here."

"She's family now; of course she'll call you Grandpa," Hunter said.

As Rennie looked between them, she realized she knew how Hunter would look when he was old. Tall, proud, still firm in muscle and tone, George Bradshaw was a hard man. One had to be to survive on Australia's rugged outback.

But he looked fair. She hoped he wouldn't condemn her out of hand just because of her looks.

"And this is Kerry, I'm sure," Rennie said, smiling shyly at the little girl.

"Couldn't have two babies. This one is enough to wear us all out. Say g'day to the pretty lady, honey," George said to Kerry, his expression softening immediately.

Clearly he loved his great-granddaughter.

"Will she let me hold her?" Rennie asked, holding out her arms. Kerry leaned over toward Rennie, her expression solemn, her brown eyes wide and searching.

"No!" Hunter said.

Too late. The little girl plopped against Rennie, hugging her and wrapping her dirty legs around Rennie's hip.

Rennie swung around to stare at Hunter. Should she move more slowly in trying to get to know the baby?

"She'll get your clothes dirty," he explained.

"They'll wash. She's adorable."

Hugging the child close, something unexpected happened to Rennie.

She fell in love.

Studying the little girl's wide-eyed stare, she smiled, her heart expanding for the love and delight she'd take in this precious child. All her doubts and confusions fled instantly. She'd been right to come to Australia and marry Hunter Bradshaw.

She'd be a good mother to this little girl. Glancing at her new husband beneath her lashes, she wondered if she'd could become a good wife.

He was staring at her, tension shimmering between them again.

Rennie couldn't look away; she was held by the strength in his eyes, trapped by muscles that wouldn't respond to her command to move.

Finally, Hunter broke contact and left to get her luggage. She almost sagged in relief. She'd better learn to handle her reactions around him. She'd never survive otherwise.

"Come upstairs; I'll show you where you'll sleep," Hunter said when he returned a moment later.

She hadn't moved.

"Grandpa, are you still going to fix tucker tonight?"

"Sure, like always. Give Rennie a day or so to settle in. You can cook, can't you?" he asked gruffly.

Rennie nodded and turned to follow Hunter. She was starting to feel overwhelmed. She'd expected to have to deal only with Hunter and Kerry, not a crusty old man who obviously didn't want her there.

Hunter strode down the dimly lit hall in that lazy, easy way of his, carrying her bags as effortlessly as if they were empty. He paused at the bottom of the steps and let her precede him. At the top she hesitated.

"This way."

Hunter pushed open a door on the right and set her cases beside a single bed. Rennie followed, her eyes taking in the room, as bare and stark as a nun's cell. The bed had sheets and a blanket, no coverlet. There were shades on the windows, no curtains. A scarred dresser stood against one wall. That was all.

Not even a bedside light for reading, she thought in dismay as she looked thoughtfully at the lone ceiling fixture. Good thing her Kindle was back lit. She liked to read before falling asleep.

"Kerry's room is next door and Grandpa's is beyond. I'm across the hall. The bath is the second door on the left."

"This is fine," she said brightly.

He looked around the sterile room as if seeing it for the first time.

"You might want to fix it up a little."

She nodded, afraid to offend. It needed to be fixed up a lot.

He hesitated as if to say something more, but then shrugged and moved toward the door.

"Dinner's at six-thirty. You can get settled until then. Starting tomorrow, I hope you'll prepare the meals."

Rennie stayed where she was, listening to his footsteps recede as he descended the stairs and headed back to the kitchen. Then silence.

The baby stared at her. She hadn't said a word.

"Want to watch while I unpack?" Rennie asked, rewarded when Kerry smiled and nodded.

By the time Rennie had put away her clothes, found the bathroom and washed Kerry, she was exhausted. She hadn't found many clothes for the baby, so had dressed her in a clean cotton T-shirt and fresh diapers.

At least Kerry looked neat and tidy now.

Fatigued from the tensions of the day, and the different time zones she'd so recently traversed, Rennie settled Kerry with her on her bed and lay down beside her. She'd rest a few minutes and then explore the house.

Closing her eyes, she could hear the gentle rustle of the leaves in the tall trees through the open window, feel the soft warmth of the scented air brush against her skin. It was peaceful, calming, soothing.

"Rennie?"

A roughened hand gently brushed a tendril of hair off her cheek, lingering a moment, warm against her soft skin. Hard fingers tangled in her hair, combing through the tresses. The voice was dark and deep and compelling. Her skin quivered at the touch.

"Mmm?"

Floating, she kept her eyes closed, wanting to enjoy the unexpected sensations, afraid they'd disappear if she woke up.

"Rennie, wake up. It's time to eat."

Hunter's voice was low, seeping into the corners of her mind like fine wine. His hand brushed against her cheek again, moved to settle against her neck, warm and hard, yet gentle as his thumb caressed her jaw.

Rennie slowly opened her eyes. He was leaning over her, his face close to hers, his silvery eyes watching her as she came awake. Cherishing the feel of his hand against her skin, Rennie moved her head, trying to capture him against her shoulder. His thumb brushed her jaw again, sending tingling shafts of sensitivity through her whole body.

She'd never felt like this before. Of course she'd never been awakened by a virile man in her room either. It somehow seemed intensely intimate.

"Wake up," he said again, his smile lazy as he watched her come awake.

His eyes became hooded. His dark hair was brushed away from his face, growing long, brushing his collar.

Rennie stared up at him, wondering if she was still dreaming. Her fingers longed to brush through his hair as his hands had brushed hers. To feel the thickness, the texture. It was so dark and she wanted to see it against her pale skin.

"Is it late?" She looked around. "I didn't mean to fall asleep."

She couldn't think. She could only feel Hunter's hand on her skin, feel a longing rise within her that cried out to be assuaged. The intensity of her feelings was scary.

"Time to eat. I came in and got Kerry a little while ago. She's downstairs. Grandpa has everything ready."

She nodded and slowly sat up. He stepped back, reaching out to take her hands and pulling her to her feet. He seemed to tower over her. She was conscious of her bare feet.

"I'll be right down," she said, suddenly self-conscious, standing so close to Hunter, her hands in his.

His blatant masculinity filled her senses with robust sensuality. The room seemed to shrink and air was difficult to pull into her lungs. She could feel the strength in his grasp, the hard calluses from the work he did, the strong fingers that held hers so gently.

Afraid of where these profound longings might lead, she tugged her hands free.

"I'll be right down," she repeated.

What was so unique about this man that she was drawn so powerfully to him? She stepped back. He wasn't looking for anything like that from her. They had a business arrangement.

His face hardened slightly at her actions and his smile faded, but he merely nodded and turned to the door.

"We'll wait."

When Rennie entered the kitchen a few minutes later, George and Kerry were seated on one side of the table,

Hunter on the other. Hunter pulled out the chair beside him.

Flustered, she hastened to take the seat he offered.

She ate quietly as the men discussed the day's events on the station, Hunter asking questions, George replying. Listening carefully to their exchange, she was pleased at all she understood. She knew a lot about cattle and easily followed their discussion.

"Did you get unpacked?" Hunter asked, abruptly changing the subject and swinging his attention to his new wife.

Rennie nodded.

"Find every thing you need?"

"Yes. Except for Kerry's clothes."

He looked across at the little girl and then back at Rennie.

"She's dressed in a clean shirt so you must have found them."

"Where's the rest of her clothes? I only saw shirts in the drawers."

"She outgrew the ones Tessa had for her. So I just got her T-shirts. It's hot here."

"Maybe I could pick up a few things for her at the store in town," Rennie murmured. "Or order on-line if I know her size."

She didn't want to insult her new husband, but a baby girl needed more than just T-shirts.

"Maybe you two should have waited on that marriage," George said. "She's not here five hours and already talking about going back into town. I tell you Hunter, she won't last. Marjorie's will was foolish in the extreme and your going along with it was bad enough to begin with, but when a pretty girl like that shows up it makes your plan just plain impossible. I thought you would have learned your lesson before. She won't stay for the long haul."

Rennie couldn't ignore his comments. How dared he talk to Hunter as if she weren't present?

"I thought you said this arrangement would last until one of us dies," she threw at Hunter, her pride rearing up.

She remembered what he'd said earlier–would he restate it before his grandfather?

"I did." Hunter's expression was closed, his lips tight with disapproval. "We are married now and will stay married."

His anger was directed at his grandfather.

"Bloody fool," George muttered.

Hunter's anger blazed as he faced the older man.

"I don't need any advice at this stage, Grandpa. Rennie and I have made a bargain, and I expect both of us to keep it."

The resemblance between the two hard men was never more evident than when George's temper flared to match Hunter's.

"Well, maybe you should listen to a wiser man. Your mother barely lasted five years. Tessa stayed less than two. What do you think this young miss will do? She only married you for the money. Once she has that, there's nothing to hold her here."

"We know what we're doing. An arranged marriage is like a business arrangement and maybe better suited to the kind of life we have out here," Hunter retorted.

Rennie felt the waves of his anger, yet she knew of the tight control Hunter kept on his emotions. He was right, there wasn't any love between them–it was a purely business marriage.

For a confused moment she wondered what it would be like to have Hunter love her. He was clearly a man of strong emotions. She could feel the anger raging in him. What if he loved as strongly?

She blinked. She didn't believe in love. Not from a man. She was too leery of ever giving her heart again. She refused to open herself up to such hurt, nor constantly seek the will-o'-the-wisp the way her mother had.

"You don't know her," George snapped.

"Neither do you," Rennie broke in, tired of being treated as if she weren't present. "And neither do I know Hunter, but I trust him when he says it will work out. What should we have in this marriage—love? That's an overrated emotion that has no staying power. I should know—my mother was in and out of love dozens of times, married seven times. None lasted. You don't think I have any staying power—well, I don't think much of men's protestations of love. They say anything to ensnare a woman, then leave her bleeding—"

George broke in, "My Anna loved the station, worked with me to build it up. We had a lot of love between us. She died young, when Hunter's father was just a boy. I never wanted another woman after her. Pete's wife, on the other hand, couldn't take life on the station. She left after a few years. And Alex didn't fare any better–Tessa only stayed two years."

"And complained the entire time," Hunter added, his temper eased.

"But I'm not Hunter's mother, nor Tessa. I'm Rennie, and I plan to stay."

"We'll see, won't we?" George said, eyeing her balefully.

Rennie was almost shaking in the aftermath of the emotions that surrounded the table. Were all dinners like this? Or was this one special to celebrate her arrival?

"Don't let Grandpa get to you," Hunter said when the old man left the room. "He's still hurting over Alex."

She nodded, wishing her arrival had gone more smoothly. Still determined to make the most of her new life, however, Rennie refused to let George's attitude bring her down. She'd promised to stay married to Hunter, and she meant to keep that promise, no matter how hard, or what the provocations around her were. She refused to be like her mother, nor Tessa, nor Hunter's mother. Of that she was resolved.

During the next two days Rennie explored her new home, cared for Kerry and prepared the meals.

Hunter worked from breakfast to supper.

When he was gone, she was almost able to forget about the swirling undercurrents that rippled around them when they were together. But when he sat at the table and looked at her she had a hard time ignoring them.

Each day she'd lecture herself on how to behave, and follow through outwardly. But inside she trembled with unexpected strain. It was due to hormones, or the time-zone changes, or living below the equator after a lifetime above, she told herself.

As soon as she was used to him, she reactions would calm down.

Trying to distract herself from the growing compulsion that Hunter was becoming, she threw herself into plans to make the house a home for them all. There were no signs of a woman's touch anywhere. The curtains in the living-room were old and faded.

The rooms were furnished with the minimum of utilitarian furniture. No pictures hung on the walls, no knick-knacks softened the tables. There were books everywhere, as if the men dropped them where they read them.

Had Tessa contributed nothing?

Or had all signs of her presence been erased?

Planning how to decorate the house, bring color and comfort into each of the rooms filled Rennie's time.

Every waking moment, she grew to know the baby better. Kerry followed her around and sat on the counter to "help" when Rennie prepared the meals.

She tried dusting when Rennie cleaned the rooms. She was especially fond of washing, splashing in the water and getting herself and anything near by soaked.

Rennie found a small table that she moved to her room beside her bed. But there was no lamp. If she could run into town, she'd buy one. She also wanted some play clothes for Kerry, wanting to spoil the little girl who'd lost both her parents at so young an age. She wanted to buy her toys and fuss over her.

She needed to ask Hunter about going into town, but she walked warily around George, not wanting to give him any reason to start complaining about her again.

Yet in the two days she'd been there she'd only seen Hunter at meals. Once supper was over, he retired to the office with George and they discussed business until long after Rennie went to bed.

Rennie knew the only time she could be sure of privacy for her request would be at night after George retired.

3

Biding her time that evening, Rennie waited until she heard Hunter close his bedroom door. Without delay, she quietly crossed the hall from her room and knocked tentatively on his door.

He opened it, looking down at her with surprise. He'd begun to prepare for bed. His checked shirt was unbuttoned, pulled from his jeans. The copper tone of his chest was clearly visible, as was the light dusting of dark hair that covered his muscles.

"Rennie?"

"Could I talk with you?" she asked, flicking a quick glance over him, her throat drying at the tantalizing sight of so much bare skin.

For an agonizing moment she forgot why she'd come, speculating instead on whether his deep copper skin was as warm as it looked, wondering what the corded muscles showing would feel like if she touched him. She'd love to skim her hands over him, press herself against that solid strength and see what it felt like.

"Of course."

He took her arm, drew her into his room and closed the door behind her.

Stalling for a moment, unable to meet his eyes, desperately

trying for control over her wayward thoughts, Rennie looked curiously around his room. She hadn't ventured into his bedroom during her explorations.

It was almost as sparse as hers, but with a king-size bed, and a lamp beside his pillow. Beyond the bed, she could see the door to a private bathroom.

"What is it?"

Hunter waited patiently for her to speak, his hand still on her arm, his fingers now moving gently against her soft, warm skin.

Rennie's eyes widened when she felt the tug on her senses as his fingertips sent pulsing waves of delight and enchantment through her. His fingers were magic, causing wonderful warm tingling sensations deep within her.

For a brief second she tried to remember why she'd come to speak to him, caught up in the fascination that his touch wrought. Her eyes caught the heat in his, the sensual curve of his lips, and she reveled in the delightful captivated charm her body felt for his, as if it recognized it from the beginning of time. She trembled slightly as he continued to caress the sensitive skin beneath her arm.

"Rennie?"

Hunter's other hand came up to cup her chin and he lowered his head, his mouth covering hers in a warm kiss.

Shocked, Rennie remained still, ensnared by the pleasure that coursed through her at his touch. His lips were firm and warm, moving against hers until she was compelled to respond. When her lips moved with his she felt as if she was floating, meeting his light, nibbling touches that learned and taught. Then she was propelled backwards until she came up against the hard wooden door. Both his hands cupped her cheeks and he tilted her face the better to receive his kisses, his mouth covering hers completely.

Taking a breath, she parted her lips and Hunter moved to plunge into her warm moistness. His tongue teased her soft inner lip, causing her heart-rate to soar. When he traced her teeth then delved deeper to find and stroke her tongue, Rennie gripped his wrists to keep from falling. Her legs trembled with numbing weakness.

Her entire body hummed with his touch, hungering for more. She'd never been kissed like this before. Not even by Stuart. Was this the way husbands kissed? No wonder her mother had married so many times.

Heat spread throughout every cell, every nerve-ending. Her mouth moved against his, seeking more. Her tongue tentatively, shyly danced with his, the tension in her body building to overwhelming proportions.

Stuart's kisses had fallen far short. Hunter's kiss was fantastic!

When Hunter eased back a few inches, he was breathing hard. Rennie took scant satisfaction in the fact. She hadn't wanted the kiss to end at all. Helpless to move, she remained with her head cupped by his calloused palms, her own fingertips recording his pulse beat. Her eyes gazed into his. Could he read her confused longing, the desire for another kiss blazing in her look?

"I didn't expect you. At least not so soon," he said, his breath fanning her cheeks as his lips touched her eyes, her nose, each flushed cheek, his tongue flicking a quick caress to the small dimple.

"Expect me?"

What did he mean? She wanted him to kiss her again. Once again to feel that floating dizzy sensation of his mouth on hers.

"I didn't expect you in my bed so soon," he said, pulling back another inch to gaze down at her in blatant male satisfaction.

That shocked her into awareness. *No, that wasn't why she had come.* She tugged on his wrists and he eased his hands down, watching her closely, a puzzled look crossing his face.

"You're crazy. I can't jump into bed with you. I hardly know you. I've only been here a couple of days."

She was babbling, but she scarcely knew what she was saying. She wasn't sure of her emotions, but they were out of control. Good grief, he thought she wanted to go to bed with him. She did, but she shouldn't. She couldn't. She shook her head.

"That's not part of our agreement. We have a business arrangement, to fulfill the terms of the will."

She'd never considered the physical aspect. How stupid of her. Her breath caught when for an instant she imagined them in his bed, his long body covering hers, his strong, slightly rough hands caressing her, bringing her to a delight she'd only read about. She swallowed hard.

His expression changed in an instant. Irritation replaced warmth as his eyes grew hard, his lips pressed tightly, his hands balled into fists at his side.

"It's a natural process between male and female."

"What about a closer relationship first?" she demanded, shocked at the turmoil that roiled through her at his words.

"Neither one of us believes in love. We have a commitment between us–what more could you want?"

"A lot more!" she almost yelled.

Blast it all, she hadn't expected to be so physically attracted to Hunter.

"Then why are you here?" he asked.

"I came to see if I could go into town tomorrow and get a few things. You said I'd have use of a car. I don't even have a lamp beside my bed to read with. And Kerry can't wear T-shirts all her life."

She remained near the door, afraid that her legs wouldn't hold her if she tried to move. She kept her eyes locked with his, afraid of what she'd be tempted to do if she gazed at his lean body, so sexily displayed by the open shirt. Afraid of what would happen if she gave into the overwhelming urge to run her fingers across that muscular body and offer herself up to his kiss again.

When Rennie realized he was listening to the echoes of his grandfather's words, she tilted her chin.

"I'm trusting you not to kick me out now that you can get your share of the inheritance, and I think you need to start trusting me that I won't leave like Tessa did."

She spoke more sharply than was necessary, but it was the result of the hectic rush of emotions still racing through her.

Or was it to cover up the desolation she felt to be separated from him?

He turned and walked to the dresser. Picking up a set of keys, he tossed them to her.

"These are for the Land Rover in the shed beside the barn. It's yours. Next time you come in here, be prepared to stay!"

Rennie whispered a thank-you. Before she could turn to flee for the safety of her own room, his eyes raked her.

"You're a pretty woman, Rennie. A man would have to be a monk or a saint not to want to sleep with you. And I'm neither. After your response tonight, I don't plan to wait too much longer to consummate this marriage of ours."

With a quick gasp, she turned and was gone.

She was ages falling asleep. Over and over she relived every moment of their kisses. At least she knew he was as attracted to her as she was to him.

"A natural process between male and female."

Was that all he felt? Could she make love to someone she didn't even know?

Yet he was right—she didn't trust love. He was outspoken against it. Where did that leave them?

The next morning Rennie's attention wasn't on the road even though she was driving on the left for the first time and sitting on what she felt was the wrong place for the steering wheel. Kerry was in the baby carrier in the back seat babbling softly.

There was no traffic, and it was a good thing, because Rennie could hardly concentrate on driving. She was still reliving the hot kisses Hunter had given her last night, as she had constantly since she'd left his room. She'd never expected his touch to be so devastating. Never expected to respond so wildly, to crave caresses from a man she scarcely knew and didn't love.

She blinked, tried to force the image away, but to no avail. It dominated her thoughts.

She wanted to spend more time with him, learn all she

could about the man who was now her husband.

Wanted to see what she could do to make her special to him, to have him be glad he'd married her.

Was she falling in love with him?

That thought dashed the memory of his kisses from her mind. No. She refused to let herself be caught up in that fickle emotion. Not for her the same route her mother had claimed each time she'd found someone new. Not for her the chance of searing pain that she'd known when she'd realized Stuart didn't love her, but had only used her.

She'd admire Hunter, respect him and like him, maybe even let herself crave his touch, but that was purely physical.

She would *not* fall in love!

And no more thinking about his kisses. She had a list of things she wanted to buy in town. Her plan was to purchase everything quickly and return to Silver Creek Station. She hadn't told George where she was going, and didn't want to be gone so long that she couldn't have dinner ready on time.

She remained uncomfortable around George and avoided him whenever possible. He continued to make predictions of her early departure, grumbling daily because Hunter had married her.

If he was trying to drive her away, he was going about it the wrong way. Each time he passed a comment it only strengthened her resolve to remain, if only to spite him.

Hunter hadn't stopped George's snide comments as he had the first night. But Rennie didn't need him to fight her battles. She was satisfied with their bargain.

Or would have been if last night had never happened.

He'd been very plain. She shivered, remembering the hot

desire in his eyes, the firmness of his jaw. She'd thought she loved Stuart and had enjoyed sex with him, but his touch had not burned as Hunter's did. Her body never craved his touch.

Hunter wanted her. She was the one keeping them apart. If he kissed her again, there was a real danger that she'd go up in flames and give in in an instant. Her best course would be stay away from him.

The metallic roof of the department store showed in the distance, the tallest building in Boolong Creek. Driving over the narrow wooden bridge that spanned a dry culvert, Rennie began to feel nervous again.

She hadn't met anyone in town beside the minister who had married them, and his assistants who had served as witnesses. Boolong Creek was a small community. Surely by now everyone knew that Hunter Bradshaw had taken a foreign wife. Did they know she was virtually a mail-order bride?

Suddenly Rennie wished she'd discussed the situation with Hunter. She didn't want to say the wrong thing.

But he probably didn't care what others thought. She'd never met such a confident individual before. He made his own way and apologized to no one for it.

Because of her uncertainty, Rennie held herself apart from the friendliness offered her by the clerks in the department store. She was polite but distant and as a result discouraged questions.

The curiosity of the man at the post office wasn't as easily dampened, but Rennie was noncommittal in her responses and escaped with a stack of mail for the station, and a note from Gram.

She needed to find out from Hunter exactly what he

wanted her to tell people before she ventured in again.

"Mrs. Bradshaw, I presume?"

A tall man dressed in a constable's uniform approached Rennie as she was strapping Kerry into her baby seat.

"Yes?"

She smiled politely, wondering if she'd parked illegally. Unless she missed her guess, this was the local law.

"Gerry Dalton. I'm a friend of Hunter's. Welcome to Boolong Creek."

"How do you do, Mr. Dalton? How did you know who I was?"

Rennie was touched that a friend of Hunter's should seek her out and introduce himself. Gerry was as tall as Hunter, but looked less substantial. He had light brown hair and hazel eyes and his skin was not nearly as tanned as Hunter's.

"Word travels fast around here. Do you have time for a cuppa?"

"Thank you but not today. I want to get Kerry home before she becomes fretful."

"Next time you're in town, then. Tell Hunter I'll drop by one afternoon."

Gerry took her refusal in stride and nodded genially as he moved down the sidewalk.

As she drove from town, Rennie thought she'd better make up a batch or two of cookies to have on hand in case they had visitors drop in. Did Hunter do much entertaining? There were so many things she didn't know about him, about what he expected from their marriage.

Kerry had behaved beautifully and Rennie was pleased that the child was so easy to take with her. Because of the dearth of toys at the station, Rennie bought her a rag doll and a set of blocks. Kerry played with the dolly on the ride home, babbling to it and waving it around holding it by its hair. All in all Rennie was pleased with their outing.

George was working in the office when Rennie arrived home. She handed him the stack of mail she'd picked up without a word. Taking the bags of purchases up to her room, she had to pass by the open door. He looked up, taking in the boxes and bags of things as she hastened up the stairs. He made no offer to assist, merely looked up each time she passed by, noting the number of trips she made.

Rennie was excited. She brought Kerry up to the baby's room and talked to her as she began putting away the clothes she'd bought for her.

"You'll look adorable in this yellow play suit. Won't Hunter and Grandpa be surprised at dinner? Here, honey, you can play with these blocks. Look, we'll stack them... Oops." Rennie laughed when Kerry shoved over the tower. "I guess that's how you play with blocks when you're not yet two."

Closing the last drawer in Kerry's chest, Rennie bundled up the bags and tossed them near the door. "Now the good part, sweetie. Look at these curtains. They have rainbows and sunshine on them. Do you ever see rainbows here? And here's a matching comforter for your crib. Doesn't that look nice?"

Rennie could hardly wait to put up the curtains, but she'd need Hunter's help. There were no rods in place and she didn't know where any tools were kept. She'd bought all she needed for the room. He'd have to spend a little time helping her put up the rods.

For a moment she let herself imagine them working

together, talking, learning more about each other. Acting like a real married couple. A true family.

Stunned at where her thoughts were leading, she turned back to finish opening the bags.

Spreading out the fluffy scatter rugs, Rennie surveyed the room in satisfaction. It already looked better with the added color. She'd also bought wallpaper that matched the curtains for the wall between her room and Kerry's. And paint for the trim. She could handle that herself.

Time to start dinner. She didn't want to be late and give George anything to complain about. Taking Kerry and her new toys, Rennie hurried to the kitchen.

Promptly at six-thirty she dished up the meal. The men had already washed and were sitting around the table. Smiling pleasantly, Rennie placed the large platter of fried chicken before George. Adding the bowl of peas, potatoes and beets, she whisked the biscuits from the oven and set them on the table.

Sitting beside Hunter, she watched anxiously to see if everyone liked the meal. It was a typical meal in Texas, but she'd only served beef since her arrival at Silver Creek Station. Would they like the chicken?

"Thought you'd have on new clothes tonight," George said, eyeing her regular jeans and lightweight cotton vest-top.

"Why?" Rennie asked, puzzled by his comment. "Was tonight special?"

"Saw you couldn't wait to get away from the station today. Went into town, right? Here only three days and already had to get out."

She nodded cautiously. She'd gone to town, but not

because of cabin fever, nor to purchase anything for herself except the lamp and some paint.

George watched her through narrowed eyes.

"Saw all the parcels you brought up. Must have bought out the store."

He looked at Hunter.

"She'll bankrupt you in no time at that rate."

"I didn't buy any clothes. At least not for myself. I did get Kerry a few things," Rennie said quietly.

Had no one noticed the new play suit she was wearing?

"You made at least six trips up the stairs, loaded down every time."

"You keeping score?" Hunter asked, his voice hard.

"Dammit, when are you going to realize she doesn't belong here? She'll run you ragged, spend your money, then leave."

Rennie put her hand on Hunter's arm, forestalling his reply.

"I bought some things to fix up my room and Kerry's. And I used my own money."

"You've no call for that!" George snapped. "What's the matter, Missy, this house not good enough for you?"

"This is her home and she can fix it up however she wants. And not only her room and the baby's. If she wants to change any of the other rooms, she can," Hunter replied.

"It isn't your house!" George's grim tone challenged.

Hunter became still, his eyes hard as he gazed at his grandfather, dinner momentarily forgotten.

"No, it's not my house, but it is my home and my wife's home. If you don't want us to treat it as such, just let me know. I'll build another."

His voice was deadly calm.

There was a shocked silence. Time seemed to stop.

Rennie held her breath, her eyes darting between the two strong men. She hadn't meant to precipitate a crisis.

Then George slowly shook his head.

"No, I don't want you to move."

"So Rennie can fix it up to suit herself," Hunter clarified.

"Yes."

"Rennie's my wife, Grandpa, and you need to accept that. I won't stand for any more interference or badgering. If we can't live here in harmony, I'll move us out. But Kerry goes with us."

Hunter's hard glare nailed his grandfather and for a long moment no one moved or spoke.

Rennie's heart began to beat faster at his words. They might only have a business arrangement for a marriage, but Hunter was standing up for her, siding with her. She began to believe that she'd never need to worry about his leaving like her mother's husbands. Or betraying her like Stuart.

She was almost giddy with the feelings that assailed her. He'd stood up for her against his own grandfather. And he had only known her three days. She'd never forget that.

"Not my bedroom and not the office," George said at last, conceding defeat.

Rennie nodded and dropped her gaze to her plate, wanting to shout for joy at the happiness that surged through her. She'd make the house a home for all of them. But slowly, so that the men didn't feel threatened.

And only her room and the baby's would be frilly and feminine. The rest she'd make comfortable and relaxing, but strive to hold the masculine tone.

"What did you buy today?" Hunter asked her as the tension eased around the table.

She told him, explaining her plans for Kerry's room and her own.

"So I can do everything myself, except I'll need your help with the curtain rods," she finished, unaware how earnest yet uncertain she looked when asking for his help.

"We'll do it after dinner," he said.

"I'll come by later and see the transformation. A little girl needs some frilly things," George said, as if trying to make amends.

Rennie was grateful to him for trying. It couldn't be easy for him to have her suddenly thrust into their midst. She hoped in time they'd learn to deal together, after she learned to deal with her husband. She knew little more about Hunter now than she had that first day. But as George had said, it was still early days.

When dinner was finished, Rennie washed the dishes while George took Kerry for a walk to see the horses. Hunter sat at the table, lingering over his coffee, watching his wife clean the kitchen. She was aware of his regard and slowed her movements to keep from being clumsy with nerves.

The memory of his kisses shimmered around her. She rather thought she preferred his disappearance to the office to his sitting and staring at her. She was relieved when they headed upstairs to the baby's room.

"Did you get all the hardware we need to hang these rods?" Hunter asked, striding into Kerry's bedroom, tool box in hand. His boots sounded loud on the wooden floor.

Rennie pulled the hardware from the package and nodded.

"So the man at the store told me."

As she glanced up, her heart caught. He looked so masculine standing among baby things, so out of place in the little girl's room. His hair was thick and wavy, deep dark brown in color. His shoulders were broad, his long legs planted as he eyed the window-frame. She felt that curious tingling sensation being around him, and wondered if he felt anything similar when around her.

Standing, she handed him the curtain rod brackets, careful to keep from touching him. She'd go up in flames if she did.

"I like what you've done so far," he said, surveying the room. "A little girl needs a woman around." His voice was reflective.

Rennie looked away. The images of their kisses last night arose again unbidden and she had trouble remembering what they were doing in Kerry's room. She handed him the support pieces, dropping them into his outstretched hand.

Measuring, marking, hammering, Hunter worked quickly and efficiently and in only a few minutes the curtains were in place. Bright and cheery, they added warmth and color to the room.

"Nice," he said, his roughened hands tracing down the ruffly edge.

"I wanted to get something that could last until she's about ten or twelve and can decide what she wants herself. This isn't too babyish, do you think?"

"No. But feminine."

Hunter turned to her, his eyes roaming her face.

Rennie caught her breath. Her insides began to melt and the now familiar heat rose. She couldn't move, couldn't take her gaze from his. Suddenly she felt that floaty sensation again.

"You're very feminine yourself," he said softly, his finger tracing a line of fire down her cheek, down her throat, to the soft edge of her scooped-neck cotton vest-top.

Rennie swallowed hard, almost trembling at his touch, at the emotions that tumbled through her. Her gaze flickered to his mouth, wondering if he'd kiss her again like last night. She yearned to feel his lips against hers, feel the wash of sensation that flooded her at his touch, and it was all she could do to keep from flinging herself into his arms and begging for another of his hot, erotic kisses.

"Thank you for standing up for me tonight," she said softly.

She needed to shake the spell that threatened. This was a perfect private time to let him know how grateful she was for his support.

"You're my wife," he said, his finger tracing the edge of her top from shoulder to shoulder.

Her skin burned where he touched her.

"I meant what I said. If we can't be happy here, we'll build a place of our own."

"But your grandfather..."

"My grandfather is still hurting over Alex. And he's afraid for me. He doesn't have much faith in marriage and doesn't believe ours will endure. I hold what I have, Rennie. Make no mistake, I won't let you go, even if you beg me."

His hands gripped her shoulders as he made his vow.

She shook her head.

"I don't want anything different, Hunter." She tilted her head, considering. "I don't feel very married. Somehow I thought I'd feel different. I guess it's because the house was here all along and I'm a newcomer."

"So fix it up as you wish."

His eyes darkened slightly, his silvery gaze heating her the way a candle might.

His hands moved to her waist and slowly he pulled her closer.

"What money did you use to buy these things?" he asked as he drew her close enough to feel the warmth from his body. "From your share of the inheritance?"

"No, I don't have that yet. I used my charge card," she said breathlessly, almost unable to answer coherently.

Every inch of her was aware of him, from his strong legs, spread slightly apart, to his narrow hips and broad chest. The seething heat from him met her own glow and threatened to ignite her.

Hunter frowned.

"I'll pay for anything you buy."

"Because we're married I assumed everything I had would be yours. Except the money I need for Gram. Why would we need separate accounts?"

Her hands opened against his chest, and slowly she rubbed her fingertips against the cotton-sheathed muscles.

His eyes searched hers and then he nodded.

"We don't. But in the future charge things at the stores in town on the stations' account. We have an account at each one. Just tell them you're Mrs. Hunter Bradshaw."

He said it arrogantly, and she smiled involuntarily. Did everyone in Boolong Creek bow and scrape for Hunter Bradshaw and therefore his wife?

"Yes, I'll tell them that."

For the first time she almost felt married and it was curious. She thought she liked it.

The door bounced against the wall with the force of opening. George stood in the doorway glaring at them.

"I thought you came up to hang curtains," he said, taking in Hunter's hands at Rennie's waist, her glowing face.

"Done."

Hunter released Rennie and bent down to retrieve his hammer and tape measure.

"Hmmph! You need to know Daphne wants to come for a visit."

Hunter's head shot up. "Daphne Adams?"

"She wants to see Kerry, discuss the custody issue. She says she's coming on behalf of her parents. I'm sure her plan is to take Kerry back to Sydney with her."

"Well, she bloody well can't. I spoke to our attorney on the phone two days ago and told him about my marriage. He assured me that would be enough to be awarded custody. I've started adoption proceedings," Hunter said, starting toward the door.

"Who's Daphne?" Rennie asked, feeling left out.

"She's Tessa's sister," George said. "Kerry's aunt. And she wants to come visit her niece. So she says. I bet she's here to see you, Hunter."

Hunter frowned. "I doubt it–that was over ages ago."

"What was over?" Rennie asked softly, almost afraid to hear the answer.

"Daphne made a big play for Hunter when Alex was courting Tessa. I thought for a while it would be a double wedding," George said with relish, his eyes on Hunter as if trying to gauge his reaction.

"But it wasn't. That's in the past," Hunter said, pushing his way through and heading down the stairs.

Rennie stood still, listening to the sound of Hunter's steps.

When he'd left, George looked at her.

"It would have made a better match. Daphne is Kerry's aunt, Hunter's her uncle. There's a blood tie there."

"And she's Australian," Rennie added, beginning to see some of the reason for his antagonism.

He nodded and turned away.

4

Rennie stood still, astounded by what she'd just learned. Hunter and Daphne?

And George seemed to prefer Daphne.

Two months ago Hunter had only been the nebulous grand-nephew of her grandmother's friend Marjorie. Now they were married to fulfill a stipulation in Marjorie's will.

Suddenly Rennie realized how much she'd counted on her marriage working, lasting. She'd meant her vows when she'd said them. Hadn't Hunter said earlier that he'd never let her go? Could she depend on him?

Or if Daphne visited, would Hunter come to the conclusion that he might have made a mistake? Would he think it better if Kerry's aunt raised her with him, instead of a stranger from America?

Rennie didn't even want to think about it. Yet there was nothing to say they had to remain married. They'd fulfilled the will's stipulation. Would Daphne jeopardize that arrangement in any way?

Nothing further was said about Daphne's request to visit over the next few days and Rennie pushed the thought from her mind, spending the time happily decorating her room and Kerry's. Maybe she had worried for nothing.

The wallpaper and paint finished the baby's room and

Rennie enjoyed walking in each morning and seeing the cheerful decor and the happy baby waiting to be picked up.

Her own room she painted pale blue, with spanking white trim. The curtains she chose were ruffly white Priscilla. They framed her view perfectly. A pale blue spread with lots of white pillows added cool color to the bed. She bought a large area rug in deep navy, and several pictures that drew the eye. A dresser scarf covered the scars on the top and her crystal perfume bottles caught the sun's gleam in the late afternoon. The lamp by her bed was perfect.

Hanging the last picture, she surveyed her room with pride. It was welcoming and pretty and she was pleased with the result.

"Rennie? Where are you, girl? Come on the run!" George's urgent roar sounded from outside.

What was he doing back so early? He'd gone out with the stock men that morning and told her he'd be gone until supper. What was wrong? Hurrying from the room, she raced for the stairs.

Kerry was still napping, so it couldn't be the baby, she thought as she flew down the stairs and out through the kitchen, her heart in her throat. Thrusting open the screen door, she skidded to a halt to see Hunter dismount from his horse. His shirt was bloody, his hat was gone and he looked pale as winter snow. George stood beside him, two other stock men stood in the yard, one holding Hunter's horse.

"Hunter's been hurt," George said unnecessarily.

One sleeve was bloody and Hunter moved gingerly as if he was in pain, easing himself from his horse, holding on to the saddle for an extra minute.

"What happened?"

She hurried over to him, reaching out to assist him, shocked at his pallor. His normally tanned skin looked almost white.

"I'll be fine," he said, trying to minimize the effects of his injuries as he reached out and encircled her shoulders with his good arm, leaning heavily against her. "My horse picked up a stone and when I stopped to get it out something spooked the cattle."

"He was lucky he wasn't trampled to death," George said heavily.

His own color wasn't very good.

Rennie wondered if she'd have two invalids on her hands.

"Come inside and let me see," she urged, her hands reaching around Hunter the better to support him.

He was so much bigger than she. Her arms reached around, pressing into his ribs. She could feel his heavy heartbeat, it was slower than her own pounding pulse.

Now wasn't the time to give in to the fear that touched her at George's words. Hunter needed her help; she could worry about what might have been later.

"I can manage," Hunter protested, but he didn't remove his arm from around her shoulders, his hand biting painfully into her.

"Maybe, but I'm here now, and I can help you."

She turned back toward the house and slowly they made their way inside. Rennie maintained a veneer of strength and calmness, though internally she was shaky. Hunter had seemed invincible to her, so strong. But this accident proved he was as human as the next man and as vulnerable to injury or loss as anyone.

"I'll see to your horse," George said, remaining behind.

Hunter waved his hand in acknowledgment but continued leaning on Rennie as they entered the house.

The stairs took forever, and Rennie wondered if they should have even started up them. Reaching the second floor, she flung open his bedroom door and helped him to the adjacent bathroom. Sitting him down, she unbuttoned his shirt, appalled that her own fingers were so shaky.

"You don't need to do this, Rennie," he said. "I can wash it off, slap on a bandage and be ready to go."

"Hold still, Mr. macho male. Of course I'll help you. You're my husband, aren't you? That's what marriage is about—being there for each other."

She pushed the shirt from his broad shoulders, taking special care on his injured side.

"I guess so."

His eyes searched her face, looking for something.

"You were there for me when your grandfather got nasty, now I can do something for you. I know first aid," she said, trying to ignore the feelings that his look engendered and hoping that her first aid would be enough.

The injuries wasn't as bad as she'd feared. The bleeding had almost stopped, probably would have done already had he not had to ride in.

The cuts and scrapes were localized on one arm, though there was considerable bruising surrounded it and the left side of his chest. There was a bruise beginning to show on his jaw, too. Cleaning his arm with a soft cloth and warm water, Rennie found the antiseptic ointment and gently spread it over the abrasions.

"What happened, did the whole herd trample you?" she asked as she worked, trying to ignore the wide expanse of bronzed chest lightly covered with dark curls that dominated her field of vision. Keeping her hands firmly on the task she was doing, she resisted brushing her fingers against the strongly defined muscles so tantalizingly near. She felt the pull between them like iron to a magnet.

"Feels like it. I fell when they spooked and rushed around me and one or two got me before I could get up again."

She shuddered at the thought of his strong body beneath the sharp hooves of the stampeding cattle. He could have been hurt far worse. Even killed.

She hesitated a long moment, trying to envision this strong man dead and gone forever.

It was impossible.

"It's more scraped than cut. And the bleeding's almost stopped. I don't think you need to see a doctor," she said doubtfully.

What if it got infected?

"No, I sure don't."

His voice had recovered some of its strength.

She smiled at his reaction, so typically male, and began bandaging the arm. She was standing in the V of his thighs, close to his body, and could feel his warm breath heat her breasts. She tried to ignore her body's reaction to his proximity, daring to hope he wouldn't notice.

He was hurt, in pain. Now was not the time to think of sex.

But she couldn't help it. His skin was tight over sculptured muscles. She longed to trace those muscles on his chest, discover if the curls that covered him were soft or crisp. Feel if his flesh was hot or warm. She concentrated on his arm, the strength solid beneath the bandage.

His warmth spread from her fingers up her arms to her body, to her very center. The insides of his thighs tightened, capturing her own legs, and she felt the touch like a brand against her sensitive skin.

"Raise your arm," she said, needing to wrap the bandage around.

He complied, resting his hand against her hip. Rennie almost dropped the gauze in startled surprise. Taking a deep breath, she focused on her work, intensely aware of Hunter when his other hand moved to rest on her other hip.

She was caught. Her legs were sensitized by his touch, her hips almost melting in his hands. He only had to tighten his muscles slightly to pull her against him. To press his face against her breasts. The longing for him to draw her closer was almost uncontrollable. She could lean forward—

"Finished," she whispered, her voice no longer strong and assured.

Would he guess why?

She dared not let him suspect.

He held her before him so that she couldn't move. For balance she placed her hands on his bare shoulders. Her fingers curled against his smooth skin, gently rubbing the solid muscles beneath. Her eyes watched her hands, afraid to meet his gaze, fascinated by the feel of his hot skin beneath her fingertips. This couldn't be happening to her; she knew enough to keep her distance.

"I'll be good as new in a day or two," he said to reassure her.

"I think your shirt is done for, however."

She met his gaze and her heart stopped at the desire that raged there.

Pulling her to his good side, he sat her on his knee and reached up to cradle her head in his hands.

As he pulled her closer, his mouth closed over hers and he mumbled, "Thanks."

Rennie sighed and closed her eyes. She knew she should resist, but couldn't.

His lips were hot and firm, moving against hers in sensuous delight. Her hands shifted, caressing his shoulders, trailing to his neck, up to his thick hair. Her fingers threaded in his hair as his threaded into hers. Hunter deepened the kiss and Rennie responded, still slightly shocked at the intensity of feeling that flared between them.

"Hunter, are you all right?" George's voice was heard as he mounted the stairs.

Rennie pulled back, her eyes wide.

Hunter chuckled at her look and kissed her again, brief and hard on the mouth, before letting her stand.

"Yes, Grandpa, I'm fine."

His deep voice resounded with strength.

Rennie was across the bathroom closing the first-aid kit when George entered. He looked at his grandson and then Rennie, worry still evident in his expression.

"Scared ten years out of me when I saw you go down."

"Yes, but Ace is a good cow pony. He stood there and the cattle had no choice but to go around. I'll get dressed and be right out."

"Oh, no, you won't!" Rennie said, looking directly at him.

"You'll take it easy the rest of today and see how you feel tomorrow before you go riding off again. Besides the injuries on your arm, you look like you took a blow to the head. You have a bruise there."

Her finger lightly traced the discoloration on his jaw.

"Now see here..."

Hunter began, standing up and looking intimidating in the small confines of the bathroom.

"Do as she says, son. Women like to fuss over men from time to time. Enjoy it while you can," George said, an unexpected twinkle in his eye.

"I don't need fussing over." Hunter clenched his teeth, a muscle jumped in his cheek. "I'm not giving into some namby-pamby sheila's notion that I need to cosset myself just because of a minor mishap!"

"Minor, ha. It's more than minor. Besides, everyone needs fussing over now and then. You scared me half to death when I saw all that blood. I think you should rest now and see how you feel later," Rennie said firmly.

She was not going to risk his health for some macho notion of getting right back to work.

"Give in to it, boy. Women have to have their own way once in a while and it won't hurt you to enjoy it," George said, grinning suddenly at the sight of the pretty, delicate woman standing up to the man who towered over her.

"Do I have to look forward to this every time I get a little scratch?" Hunter asked scathingly, resisting to the last.

"A little scratch? From what I heard you almost got trampled by a stampeding herd of cattle. And yes, the next time you're injured, you can expect more of the same." Rennie faced him, her hands balled into fists on her hips, her chin firmly tilted to stare him down.

Hunter stared at her, his lips twitching as if he was trying hard not to laugh.

"Very well, come and fuss over me," he challenged, cocking an eyebrow in a brazenly flirtatious manner.

She was stuck. Her tongue wouldn't work. She could see the broad chest that she longed to touch. His hips were cocked just so, demonstrating clearly how masculine he really was. His long legs were tightly covered by the snug jeans, leaving little to the imagination. Her gaze was drawn to his lips, the same lips that had so skillfully kissed her just seconds ago. How could she resist?

"I think you should lie down, rest until dinner."

She cleared her voice. It shouldn't be so shaky.

"Better and better," he murmured, his eyes skimming down the length of her, teasing her with his look.

George chuckled when Rennie blushed beet-red at Hunter's words.

"You'll have to excuse us, Grandpa. Rennie wants to fuss over me in bed," Hunter said, moving closer, crowding her, his eyes dancing in amusement, his gaze never leaving hers. Mocking her, challenging her, daring her.

Just then Kerry called from her room. Her relief blatant, Rennie smiled broadly.

"Climb in bed, husband, dear, and Kerry and I will bring you some chicken soup."

Fleeing before he could say another word, Rennie was grateful to the baby's timely cry. Things were moving faster than she knew what to do with.

Rennie got Kerry up and settled with her blocks before she hurried downstairs to see about something for Hunter. When she returned to his room some time later with a strong pot of sweetened tea and some aspirin, he was already in bed. His dusty jeans tossed casually over a chair and his boots lying on the floor caused Rennie to pause at the doorway. Hunter leaned up against the headboard, the white sheet tucked in around his waist. His copper-tan chest was a deep contrast to the pristine white cover and Rennie almost stumbled as she moved slowly into the room. Was he wearing anything beneath the sheet that covered him?

"I couldn't find any chicken soup," she said as she set the tray down on the bedside table and poured him a mug of hot tea. She shook out two aspirin.

"Why would I want it?" he asked easily, taking the cup, and latching on to her wrist at the same time with his free hand. Tugging gently, he brought her hand to his mouth and took the aspirin directly from her palm, his tongue wetting her soft skin. He pulled her down to sit beside him, the mattress sinking slightly, tilting his hips toward her.

Rennie swallowed hard, looking at his chest. Flustered, she looked up to meet the mocking glint in his eyes over the rim of the cup as he took a sip.

"I—er—chicken soup is a time-honored treatment where I come from. If you're sick, you have chicken soup."

"Then we'll have to get some. I don't think we have any."

"No, you don't."

"We don't," he corrected sharply, his eyes narrowing dangerously. "This is your home now, Rennie."

"Right."

She smiled tightly, trying to ignore the tingling in her wrist where his fingers lightly fondled. Trying to ignore the rampant images that her mind envisioned at his touch, of his hands on her, and her response to his caresses. Afraid of the emotions, she pushed them away.

"Hunter," she said, then looked away, afraid that she'd give in to those images. "I need to go see to Kerry."

"She's fine. I don't hear her."

"She could be getting into mischief."

Rennie tried tugging her hand free, but Hunter didn't release her.

"Where's this wifely fussing over I'm looking forward to?" he asked, his voice laced with amusement.

"I...that is...Hunter, do you have anything on?"

Rennie closed her eyes and groaned softly. Good grief, she hadn't meant to blurt that. She was about as sophisticated as a butterfly. What would he think?

Hunter's chuckle snapped her eyes open and she blushed as she met the dancing lights in his steely gaze. Reaching over, he replaced the cup on the table and lifted his sheet slightly. Taking her hand, he ran it over his chest, down his side and under the edge of the sheet.

Rennie held her breath, her heart pounding so hard that she wondered if it would burst from her chest. His skin was so warm, covering the solid muscles he kept so fit by hard work. Slowly he drew her hand beneath the white sheets until she felt the cotton edge of his briefs.

Relief flooded through her as she almost sagged against him. Color stained her cheeks and she tugged her hand again, but he continued rubbing the back of her fingers against the cotton, his eyes laughing at her.

"Want to play doctor?" Hunter asked softly, drawing her hand back up to his chest and splaying her fingers across the crisp hairs that covered him.

Rennie flexed her hand unconsciously, dragging her fingertips across the hot skin, reveling in the feel of him beneath them. Catching his mocking gaze, she shook her head and laughed unsteadily, knowing he was teasing, but not knowing how to react.

"I think I've played all the doctor I want to today. You scared me to death."

"Another time, then."

"I hope not. Hunter, I was truly scared."

Her serious eyes held his. She hardly knew him, but couldn't help her reaction.

"Don't be, Rennie. I'm fine. You have to expect some injuries on a station like this. But look at Grandpa—he's still around. Alex got killed in an automobile accident in Sydney, not out here."

"You could have been killed if your horse hadn't stood there to divert the cattle," she said.

"Maybe, maybe not. Don't borrow trouble," he said. "Though I like your wifely fussing. Maybe there's more to this marriage business than I thought."

His hand touched the back of her hand as she continued to rub against his chest, sending waves of exciting sensations up her arm.

Snatching her hand back, she stood in embarrassment.

"I think you should rest now. I've got things to do."

"Running away?" he taunted.

"It's safer," she murmured, watching him warily from the safety of the doorway.

"This arm won't put me out of commission," he complained.

"Come down for dinner, then."

She backed out of the room and turned to hurry to Kerry's room, feeling as if she'd escaped a major disaster.

But there was no escape from the tingling awareness she continued to feel thinking about Hunter.

When Rennie checked on him a little later, he was sleeping soundly. She watched him for a long moment, thankful that he'd not been injured more severely. She depended upon him. Probably would more and more as their joined lives progressed. She couldn't bear to think of him hurt or worse.

By dinner, Hunter was up and dressed and joined the others around the big kitchen table. Rennie examined him as he sat down. Meeting his gaze, she looked away, conscious of the worry she knew he must have noticed, remembering his teasing in bed. He looked fit and healthy, the pallor of the afternoon gone, though the bruise on his jaw was more pronounced.

"I came to check on you earlier, but Dr Rennie there wouldn't let anyone disturb you." George's grumbling was back to normal.

Hunter smiled and watched as Rennie placed the food on the table.

"She was still fussing," he explained.

"You look a heap better now than earlier," George said.

"Feel better, but still stiff."

Rennie fussed over him a little more at dinner, serving him first, making sure he had everything he wanted, jumping up to fetch him a beer when he asked. She could tell from his amusement that he found it funny, but she wanted to do something for him and ignored his reaction.

When dinner was finished, Hunter pushed back his chair and stood up.

"Rennie, come with me. I want to see to the horse and talk to you. Grandpa, will you watch Kerry?"

"Sure."

Rennie was surprised to be so summoned and nodded, glancing around the table. "Shouldn't I finish the dishes first?"

"They can wait. Come on."

He held the screen door and she preceded him out into the early evening. Walking across the yard, she darted a quick glance at Hunter. He looked as fit as he had that morning. She could see the thickness of the bandage beneath his sleeve, but beyond that he looked normal. It obviously took a lot more than that little stampede to keep him down.

They entered the barn, the scent of hay and horses overriding that of dust and the pungent odor of the gum trees filling the air.

Rennie breathed deeply and smiled. She always liked the smells around a ranch. If she closed her eyes, she could be back in Texas. She was just the tiniest bit homesick.

Hunter paused by Ace's stall and studied the animal. The horse nickered softly and ambled over to push his nose against Hunter's shoulder.

"Easy, boy. Let's take a look at you."

"Did he get hurt too?" Rennie asked, peering through the rails at the large black horse.

"Yes, a few gashes. Grandpa fixed him up. But I don't think I'll take him out again until he's all healed. You were great today, partner."

Hunter patted his sleek neck as he watched Ace's movements.

"He really saved you, didn't he?" Rennie said softly, her hand stroking the horse's warm nose.

A rush of gratitude filled her for the well-trained horse. She could have lost Hunter today if Ace had bolted. What would have happened to her if she had? What would have happened to Kerry?

"Come on."

Hunter reached out and took her hand, leading her over to a stack of hay and sitting pulling her down beside him on a bale.

"I wanted to talk to you privately and we can't do that with Grandpa around."

Rennie nodded, remembering that she'd gone to his room when she'd wanted to talk privately. And look where that had ended up.

"I want to give in to Daphne's request for a visit. I want her to see that Kerry will be well cared for here, by us, so she can report back to her parents. Daphne is Kerry's aunt. I don't want to keep that side of Kerry's family from her. So they can visit whenever they wish. I don't want Kerry going to live with her grandparents, however. So it's safer to have them come here than me take Kerry for a visit."

Rennie's heart dropped slightly. She remembered what George had told her—that Hunter and Daphne had once dated. Was that the real reason he wanted her to visit?

What if Hunter found he was still attracted to Kerry's aunt when she arrived? Would he change his mind about their business marriage?

It would be easy enough to annul.

What would that do to her share of the inheritance?

How could she leave Kerry?

"Rennie?"

She looked up, trying to put a bright smile on her face.

"Whatever you want, Hunter. It's your home. I'll do my best to make her welcome."

"It's our home," he said sharply. "Most of the entertaining will fall to you. I'll be working during the day. You'll have her underfoot all day."

Her smile became genuine. Underfoot didn't sound like an interested man.

"How long will she stay?"

He shrugged leaning back and resting against the wooden stall side.

"I don't know. Not more than a week I expect."

"What does she like to do?"

"As I recall, she liked to look at fashion magazines. She works at some trendy boutique near the opera house in Sydney."

His hand reached out to tug the ribbon from her hair. When it sprang free, he twirled a strand of blond curls between his fingers.

Rennie could scarcely breathe. His attentions were too distracting. How could she concentrate on their conversation when her whole being was focused on someone caressing her hair? Her heart began thumping and the blood roared in her ears.

It wasn't fair, either. He looked totally unaffected, while her whole being was linked to him by that small strand of hair he kept rubbing between his fingers.

"Er, we might not have a lot in common," she said breathlessly, resenting her reaction.

It meant nothing to him, Why couldn't she stay aloof as he did?

"Probably not." His voice was soft, soothing, cajoling. "She's never been here on the station; I only saw her in Sydney. She likes parties and nightclubs and trendy clothes. You don't seem to care much about things like that."

Rennie's gaze locked with his. Shaking her head slightly, she sighed and licked her lips, conscious that Hunter's gaze dropped to her mouth, followed the tracing touch of her tongue. She felt as if he'd touched her there. She wished he'd stop..

Or come closer.

"Should we have a party for her while she's here?" Rennie asked, mesmerized by the growing gleam in Hunter's silvery eyes.

"We'll see about a barbecue. I can give you a list of neighbors and friends to invite."

"Oh, I forgot. I met one of your friends in town the other day. Gerry Dalton."

Hunter's hand went still and his expression changed instantly. His eyes narrowed and his look became almost hostile.

"Gerry Dalton?" he repeated.

She nodded, uncertain at the abrupt change.

"He said he was a friend of yours."

"How did you meet him?"

"He stopped me at the car and introduced himself. He seemed very nice."

Was something wrong? Hunter seemed to withdraw.

"Stay away from him."

"What? Why? Isn't he a friend of yours?"

"He used to be. I want you to stay away from him."

"But why?" Rennie was puzzled by his curtness.

"He's—"

Just then a loud high-pitched scream pierced the somnolent air, followed by loud childish crying.

5

Rennie leaped up and ran from the barn, seeking the source of the crying, Hunter at her side. It came from the front of the house. Kerry was shrieking, tears coursing down her chubby cheeks. She was held tightly by George who was trying to soothe her.

"What happened?" Rennie asked as she reached for the crying baby.

Kerry lunged for Rennie and held tightly around her neck. The shrieking subsided and she cried as if in pain.

"Something stung her—bee probably," George said, picking up her foot and looking at the small white area visible in the dusty skin.

"Let's get you cleaned up and looked at, honey," Rennie crooned as they hurried into the kitchen.

In only minutes, her foot was bathed and Hunter pulled out the small stinger that had caused the problem. Kerry didn't stop crying, however. And her skin grew blotchy.

"Is she going to be all right?" Rennie asked, rocking her back and forth as she tried to stem the baby's crying.

She brushed the tears away and studied her face, not liking the look of the blotches.

"I think so. I'm going to get some antihistamine for her. Try to get her to stop crying."

Disappearing for an instant, Hunter soon returned.

Crushing the pill in a spoon, he added some water and held it for Kerry to take. She was reluctant, but he coaxed her and soon she swallowed the medicine. Her lids were growing puffy, whether from crying or from an allergic reaction Rennie wasn't sure. Soon she was wheezing.

"Hunter, she sounds worse. Should we call a doctor?"

"Nearest one is an hour or so away, in Boolong Creek. I think the antihistamine will work, we just need to give it some time. Maybe a cold cloth on her face would help."

Rennie felt a touch of apprehension at how quickly Kerry was reacting to the bee sting. But Hunter remained calm and confident. Taking strength from him, she took the wet, cool cloth he offered and bathed the baby's face.

"We need a rocking chair," Rennie said as she sat with Kerry on a kitchen chair and rocked her back and forth.

"Another remedy from Texas?" Hunter asked softly as he hunkered down beside Rennie, his hand on her hip. "I think she'll be fine. Give the medicine a chance to work."

"And if it doesn't?"

"Then we call the doctor."

"It's not as easy being out this far as I thought. I never considered how far medical care was."

Twice in one day it had been needed. In Texas her doctor had been less than five minutes away.

But she wasn't in Texas any more. And here the nearest doctor was an hour away.

"You said you had first-aid training, we've all had it. We can get the flying doctor in if there's an emergency or drive to town," Hunter said as he watched the little girl crying.

"I wished we'd had that when my Anna was so sick. She wouldn't have died if we could have gotten her to a doctor sooner," George muttered.

"There, she's better already," Hunter said as Kerry's crying eased, then ceased.

She liked the attention she was getting and was soon snuggled against Rennie's breast, shyly watching her uncle.

"I think the crisis is past," Hunter said.

He stood and leaned over Rennie, brushing past her hair, which spilled over her shoulders, to whisper in her ear, "I'd like to change places with Kerry. How come your doctoring this afternoon didn't include rocking me with my head on your breast?"

Rennie blushed. She caught sight of George's speculative gaze and dropped her own, afraid that he'd heard what Hunter had said. Was he actually flirting with her?

"If the crisis is past, I'm going to the office. Call me if you need me," George said, stomping out of the room.

Rennie looked up at Hunter, a frown on her face, though she knew her eyes were dancing in amusement at his audacious question.

"You're too big to rock."

"I'd like to rock you, honey, but not in some chair. Come on, give me Kerry and you can clean up the kitchen."

"Why don't you do the dishes and I'll play with Kerry?" she said even as she lifted the little girl into his arms.

"My injury precludes it," Hunter said loftily.

She laughed and began clearing the table, her heart light and free.

"Your injury is near your shoulder, not your wrist. A little dish-washing wouldn't hurt."

"But I want time to bond with my little girl." He looked serious suddenly. "Rennie, I've already started adoption proceedings to make Kerry our child. To give her the security of knowing we'll be her parents, not just aunt and uncle."

Rennie nodded, aware that Hunter was putting another bond in place. For the future, for all time. He wasn't going to leave the way her stepfathers had done. He was nothing like Stuart.

Watching him hold the baby, she was struck by the rightness of it all. For all he was a big, strong man, he held the baby with tenderness and love.

She yearned to feel some of that tenderness and love herself. Her eyes clouded with tears and she turned away lest he see them.

Could she be falling in love with her husband? She hoped not. He'd been very clear that he didn't want a woman falling for him. And she had best remember Stuart and his betrayal. That would cool any ideas she had of thinking she was falling in love.

"So you're agreed? We'll be her mother and father?" Hunter pressed.

"Yes, I'm agreed," she said softly, beginning to run water into the sink, emotions roiling around inside her.

Hunter and Rennie played with Kerry until it was time to put her to bed. When Kerry was tucked in, they turned together and left her room, pulling the door closed.

"I called Daphne while you were putting Kerry to bed. She'll be here the end of next week," Hunter said as they walked down the hall toward the stairs.

"So soon? For how long?"

Married less than a week and she already had a house guest expected.

"She'll stay a week."

A sudden thought occurred to Rennie and she paused, looking up at Hunter, who stopped when she did. "Where will she sleep?"

He paused in the dimly lit hall and stared down at her, his expression inscrutable. Rennie's heart began beating heavily as thoughts tumbled in her head.

Then he said very deliberately, "In your room. And you'll sleep in with me."

His look challenged her to offer another suggestion. The only other rooms on the floor had no furniture in them. There was no other place for Daphne.

She couldn't look away, mesmerized by the compelling gleam in his gaze. She shook her head, her stomach instantly filled with butterflies. Shocked by the lack of reluctance on her part, she could only stare up at him, her eyes wide and uncertain as she envisioned his big bed, his body lying next to hers.

"It's important that Daphne believes we have a solid marriage. I don't want anything to come up that might jeopardize the adoption. Sleeping with me is what she'd expect. Sorry she's coming so soon, but it was bound to happen sooner or later."

He stopped, as if trying to gauge her reaction.

It made sense in some fateful way. Especially if they were to convince Daphne to leave Kerry with them.

However, making logical sense and the actual doing were two different things. She couldn't get beyond the fact that in only a few days he wanted her to share that big bed in his room.

Fantasy images spun in her brain and she could feel heat trickle through her at the thought, then panic. She wasn't ready for anything like this.

Hunter reached out and drew her against him, lowering his mouth to touch hers lightly.

"It's time we take it to the next level," he murmured against her lips, his tongue tracing hers, flicking between her lips to brush her teeth, then retreating. "It's time you knew we're together for all time," he said, trailing soft kisses across her cheeks, along her jaw, to the pulse-point at the base of her throat.

Rennie closed her eyes the better to feel the shimmering delights his mouth brought. She trembled slightly at the thought of sleeping with him. Would he make love to her? He was her husband and he had every right to make love to her. But theirs was a business arrangement, not a love match. Why change anything?

Had he thought this through?

Hunter pulled back slightly and stared at her through narrowed eyes, taking in her erratic breathing, the flush of color on her cheeks, the confusion, trepidation and desire he read in her smoky eyes.

"Do you want to wait until Daphne comes or will you come to my bed tonight?" Hunter asked, feeling her body's surrender to his touch as his arms enfolded her, molding her along the length of his tall body.

For a split-second she wanted to follow him to his room. There was nothing stopping them. She wanted to see where his questing hands would lead, find the source of the heat that burned within her, give to him some measure of what he gave to her. It would be wonderful to make love with him.

The thought shocked her. Stepping back, she stared at Hunter. She liked him, she respected him, and she desired him. But was it enough?

In a week's time it might have to be.

But tonight?

"I'd like to wait," she said softly, afraid to commit herself.

He drew in a deep breath, his hands gripping her shoulders, but he didn't argue with her. Nodding at her request, he released her and turned to walk heavily down the stairs.

Rennie remained standing, staring after him, wondering if she'd made a mistake.

When Rennie left the bathroom that night after a long soak in a warm tub, she was pleasantly relaxed and sleepy. It had been an eventful day. She hoped future days would prove less adventurous. Wearing only her gown and light robe, she still had her hair pinned on top where she'd swept it up to keep it from getting wet in the tub. She was tired.

Hunter was leaning against the wall beside her bedroom door, one foot raised against the wall. She hesitated when she saw him then walked slowly toward her room, all signs of fatigue fleeing.

As her gaze locked with his she remembered her first sight of him at the airport. He wore no hat now and his dark hair gleamed in the hall light. But the rest was the same. She was struck by his insolent pose, his flippant masculinity, his basic virility. Her eyes skimmed over him. Darn him, was he so immune to the attraction that flared that he was amused by it?

"Did you need something?" she asked, pausing by her door.

Could she really feel the warmth from his body engulf her? Surely she was too far away.

"I wanted to thank you again for taking care of me and Kerry today. You did just fine in an emergency."

His voice was soft, throaty, wrapping itself around her like velvet. The bruise on his jaw gave him a rakish air.

"I'm glad you think so. I didn't realize before how far we were from a doctor."

"We've managed fine for a number of years and we will in the future."

She nodded, reluctant to leave, yet tongue-tied and self-conscious about her shiny face and pulled-back hair.

"Do you need me to check on the bandage?" she asked.

He smiled and reached a hand up to brush a tendril of hair from her cheek, tucking it behind her ear, his fingertips igniting her skin as they skimmed across her satiny softness.

"Not now. I was proud of you today, Yank. You didn't panic but handled things like you'd been brought up here. You'll do, mate."

This time his voice was like fine wine. Rennie thought she could become intoxicated on it as the pleasure of his words washed through her, his assessment of her filling her with pride.

"We depend on ourselves out here. More so than city folks," he said, his thumb brushing over her soft lips, his finger tracing the slight dimple in her cheek.

"Because of the distance from the doctor?"

She barely knew what she was saying. She was mesmerized by the shimmering silver heat of his eyes, the exquisite touch of his thumb against her sensitized lips, the tantalizing feel of his fingertips against her bath-warmed cheek. Slowly she licked her lips.

"Right."

Straightening from the wall, he leaned over and lightly touched his lips to hers. Looking deep into her eyes, he smiled. "I think we'll make it."

Then he crossed the hall and entered his room.

She stood rooted to the spot, unable to move for endless moments. Dazed, she at last sought the comfort of her bed.

As the days passed, Rennie continued to experience a high degree of awareness when near Hunter. He'd lean casually against the wall and talk to her when she washed the dishes, and she'd have to take extra care not to drop anything.

He made sure he was there every night to tuck Kerry in when Rennie did, often catching her against him when they entered the hall and kissing her. His very presence made her feel more desirable than she ever had, but he never again mentioned her coming to his bed.

One evening as he was watching her wash the dinner dishes she glanced shyly over at him.

"Do you realize we've been married almost a week already?"

He nodded, his eyes suddenly cautious.

"Yet I feel we don't know each other any better than the day I stepped off the plane."

"We have time to learn everything. Makes life more interesting." He shrugged as he replied. "What do you want to know specifically?"

"I don't know."

A thousand questions clamored to be answered. Where should she start?

"Did you always want to run the station?" she asked as she rinsed the last of the pans.

"Yes."

Drying the pan, she looked at him expectantly.

"Just yes? Would you care to elaborate on that at all?"

He grinned. "Like how? Yes, I did?"

She frowned. "No, more like, Yes, I wanted to run the station because I love cows, or something."

"Rennie, no one could love cattle. They are stupid, ornery and a lot of trouble."

"Then maybe you like to ride the range?"

"Yes."

"Oh, Hunter, how can I learn anything if all you do is say yes?"

Frustration spilled out when he laughed at her.

Taking the dish-towel from her hand, he threaded his fingers through hers and pulled her behind him, outside, and along the graveled driveway.

"We'll take a walk and I'll tell you all you want to know. How about that?"

"Okay," she said. She didn't like him laughing at her.

"When I was growing up I thought I'd get to run the place sometime. But my father lived here when I was a boy and naturally I thought he'd take over from Grandpa and I'd follow him. Or Alex and I would follow. We worked together these last few years. But Dad left for Sydney when I went to university."

"Why? Didn't he like it here?"

"He and Grandpa are always at odds with each other. Besides, I think some of the heart went out of him when my mother abandoned him. He waited until we were almost grown and didn't need him so much, then left."

"And your mother left when you were a little boy?"

"Yes. Alex was just a baby, I was about four."

"And your grandmother was already dead by then?" she asked.

"Yes. She died before Dad married. Dad moved to Sydney to manage a shipping firm. He likes that better than dealing with cattle. He and Grandpa seem to get along better now, too. We bought controlling interest in the company a few years back. He's the one who introduced Tessa to Alex."

"I wondered how they met," she said.

"For months Alex spent more time there than here." Hunter shook his head. "Unfortunately Tessa thought living here would be more like their courtship. But it wasn't. First of all, marriage isn't like courtship. The flowers and dinners and dancing end and the real world starts."

"She missed the romance?"

"She missed the city. Alex should have realized she wouldn't fit in here. All they did was fight. She wanted him to go work with Dad. Alex loved the station, wanted to work here. They were in love, so they insisted on getting married. I think a hot affair would have been better. In the end the emotions between them drove them apart. So much for her love," he finished scornfully.

Rennie didn't know what to say. She thought of her mother and how her life had been full of turmoil and emotion, all in the name of love. Had she been like Tessa?

"Love is overrated," she concurred.

"You say that because of your mother, don't you?"

"Yes."

He tightened his lips as she responded with the same single word he'd used. Grinning impudently up at him, she dared him to complain.

"Tell me about her," he suggested.

"There's not much to tell. She's dead now."

Her voice became expressionless as she tried to push aside the hurt that thinking about her mother always caused.

"You lived with her when you grew up?" Hunter persisted.

"My father and mother were divorced when I was little and I lived with her. She was in and out of love a dozen times. Married six more times. She had custody of me but shunted me off to my grandmother's more often than not. When I left college, I made my home with Gram."

"And?"

"And what? Love is an illusion. One she constantly sought. She didn't really want me living with her. Especially when I grew older and she tried so hard to look younger than she was."

"And she's the reason you never married?"

"I am married."

Rennie longed to change the subject. She had a secret fear that she could be like her mother. She'd thought she loved Stuart, but now she was married to Hunter, and far more attracted to him than she'd ever been to Stuart.

Was she as fickle as her mother? Would she be attracted to someone else next week?

"Before us." Hunter's voice grew impatient.

"Yes. She was not exactly an ideal example of marital fidelity. She was married seven times. She stayed until things got difficult, then left. Or the husband of the month left. Love never lasted, according to her. But she's not the sole reason I didn't get married before. I was engaged once; I thought I was going to get married and live happily ever after. But he wasn't the faithful type. Lucky for me I found out before we were married, not afterwards."

Yet she had seen happy marriages. Why couldn't she have found the kind of love those marriages were based upon? If it existed.

"Who was he?"

Rennie turned, trying to see Hunter in the faint light. He sounded angry.

"His name was Stuart Williams. He was a buyer for one of the stock houses in Dallas."

"Did you love him?"

"I thought I did, but it didn't take me very long to get over him, so I don't think it was real. I was merely caught up in my emotions, I guess."

"So you've never been in love."

"Maybe there's no such thing as true love," she said bitterly, wishing she were wrong, wishing for a love so strong that she would feel cherished all her life.

Wishing for the moon would be easier, she thought sadly.

"Love is an overblown emotion supposed to bring out the best in a relationship. But it doesn't. I was engaged myself once, a long time ago. I broke it off when I found Gina in bed with another man. Maybe you and I have something in common."

"Some people have happy marriages," she said wistfully.

"Not many. Look at Alex. He was in love with Tessa but they fought all the time. She claimed to love him, but left him to find more excitement in life. My mother deserted her family because she didn't feel loved enough."

He was silent, but Rennie knew he was remembering the bewilderment of a young boy who'd loved his mother and couldn't understand her rejection.

"It's a wonder any marriage lasts," she said softly, sadly.

"Our marriage will last, because it's based on mutual need, not some fleeting will-o'-the-wisp emotion."

Her heart sped up and she threw a quick glance in his direction. It was true they had mutual needs, but there was more than just that between them. She liked being with him, awaited the end of each day to see him. Her body yearned to receive his kisses, his caresses. The few encounters between them had only whetted her appetite.

What if he grew to love her? Would their marriage be the better for it? She'd never know for she didn't think he'd risk his heart again. What he offered would be enough. It had to be.

"If we're honest with each other, we'll have a good life together, Rennie. Without all the temperamental emotions of so-called love."

She nodded, disappointed.

Maybe she was a romantic at heart. He'd been honest and she'd have to make the most of the business arrangement that would last for a lifetime.

They turned to head back to the house when Rennie saw a kangaroo in the distance.

"Is that a real kangaroo?" she asked, transfixed. She smiled broadly.

"It is. Stay away from them, they can be dangerous."

"Will it come closer?"

"I doubt it. There's more grass out there where he is and a watering hole not too far away. Keeps them away from people for the most part."

"I wish I'd brought my phone to take a picture to show Grandma," she said.

"You'll see more. They are always around," he said, reaching out to take her hand.

When they returned to the house, Hunter brushed his lips across hers and headed for the office. She watched him as he walked away, entranced by the tight jeans, his broad shoulders, and his arrogant stroll. A little love between them wouldn't have hurt, she decided.

* * *

Rennie wiped her hands along the sides of her shorts, nervous about the coming interview. She paused outside the study door and took a deep breath. She'd been on the station almost two weeks.

Since that first night when he'd been so outspoken, she'd avoided George whenever possible. Now she was deliberately seeking him out.

Taking another deep breath, she knocked on the open door, watching as he turned away from his computer and saw her in the opening. The expected scowl dropped in place when he recognized it was her.

"Can I talk to you a moment?" she asked, pleased that her voice didn't reflect how shaky she felt inside.

She didn't want to let him know how unsure he made her feel. She always put on a strong show for him.

He nodded, and pointed to a chair across from the desk. Rennie carefully closed the door behind her and went toward it.

"Private talk, huh?" George said, leaning back in his chair and studying her. "Want out?"

She shook her head and sat on the edge of the seat.

"No, I don't want out. I know you don't think I'm right for Hunter, but I'm doing my best to be a good wife for him. I'm not some silly frivolous girl here to get my share of Marjorie's inheritance and leave. I made a bargain and will stick to it. That's not why I'm here. I need to know what Hunter's favorite cake is."

George sat up at that and stared at her in astonishment.

"Favorite cake!"

"Yes. As you know, today is his birthday and I planned to make him a cake for dessert tonight. I assume you give gifts after dinner since you didn't at breakfast," Rennie said in a rush.

She kept her gaze calmly on her grandfather-in-law, but her stomach was churning. If he scoffed at her idea, she didn't know what she'd do.

"His birthday?" George shook his head. "We don't do much for birthdays," he said flatly.

"I'm not planning much. Just a cake he'd like and steaks for dinner. I know he likes those."

"Is this more of that fussing he was talking about?"

She smiled.

"It's not much, just a cake."

"It'll be more than he's ever had."

She blinked in surprise. "What do you mean?"

"Just what I said. We don't do anything for birthdays."

"Never?"

Even her stepfathers had remembered her birthday. She'd always had cake and presents and usually a few friends over for a small party.

"When he was a kid maybe, before his mother left. It's been so long I don't remember."

"Well, I want to bake him a cake and I want it to be the kind he likes the best," Rennie said firmly, rubbing her hands against her shorts again.

"Chocolate. He always orders that when we go out somewhere."

George continued to study her as if he'd never seen her before.

"You know Daphne Adams arrives tomorrow?"

She nodded. How could she forget? She was dreading it.

"You up to handling her?"

She studied at him for a moment, wondering if he'd guessed how she dreaded the visit.

"I think so," she said calmly.

She'd do her best, in any event. What more could she do? She stood, her goal accomplished.

When she reached the door, George stopped her.

"I'm going into town in a little while. I'll get you that rocking chair you mentioned the other day."

Rennie nodded, not knowing what to say. She opened the

door, leaving it ajar behind her as she started through to the kitchen. Was that a peace offering? A sudden thought occurred to her and she spun around. Poking her head around the door-frame, she caught his eye.

"Could you get birthday candles, too? For the cake?" she asked.

He nodded, turning back to his computer. For an instant, Rennie thought she saw amusement in his eyes. She was familiar enough with the signs in Hunter's eyes. She seemed to amuse him a lot.

6

Rennie made a rich dark chocolate cake with fudge frosting. Airing out the kitchen, so as not to give away her surprise, she let Kerry lick the bowl used for the frosting. Laughing at the chocolate mess the baby made, Rennie was glad Hunter didn't come home for lunch. One look at Kerry would give it all away for sure.

Rennie dressed up a little for dinner. Wearing a soft blue dress, with a large lacy collar and cuffs, she brushed her hair until it shone, then clipped it back on either side of her head, letting the waves caress her back. She was pleased with the effort as she started down the stairs.

Everyone was in good spirits at dinner and for once Rennie didn't feel any hostility directed toward her from George. He wasn't friendly, precisely, just not antagonistic. He and Hunter enjoyed the meal and were in no hurry to leave when it was finished.

"Wait here, I have something for you," Rennie said as she began to clear the dishes. George leaned back in his chair and watched Hunter, his expression speculative.

Hunter quirked a glance at him.

"Something wrong?" he asked.

"No," George answered, amusement evident in his eyes.

Rennie went into the pantry where she'd hidden the cake

and lighted the candles, her hands trembling so hard that she had difficulty getting them lit.

She hadn't put on all thirty-four, fearing to start a conflagration, but instead had merely circled the top with candles. When they were all burning, she picked up the cake and slowly carried it into the kitchen.

Glancing up, she saw the stunned expression on Hunter's face when he first saw the cake, saw that she was bringing it to him. Tears threatened at his expression, and she swallowed hard. Had he really lived so long with no birthday cake?

"Happy birthday to you," she sang softly.

George joined in when he realized she was singing, his voice sounding rusty. Kerry banged on her high-chair, gurgling a laugh at the sight of all the candles.

"Now you must make a wish and blow them out," Rennie said as she placed the cake in front of him.

Her heart lurched at his pleased expression. She was fiercely glad that she'd done this little thing for Hunter.

He blew out the candles and Kerry clapped her hands.

"How did you know today was my birthday?" he asked as he began to lift the candles from the fudge frosting.

"I saw it when we signed the marriage certificate."

She disappeared into the pantry again and emerged with a small box, wrapped in silver and white.

"This is for you, too," she said shyly.

Dropping the box beside him on the table, she moved to get plates and forks for the cake.

George rose and went into the dining-room, returning with three more gaily wrapped presents, placing them beside Rennie's.

"A few more," he said gruffly, resuming his seat.

A hint of color stole into Hunter's dark cheeks as he surveyed the boxes before him. Slowly he raised his gaze and looked at his grandfather, then Rennie, his expression closed.

She didn't have a clue what he was thinking, but the stain of color in his face touched her and her heart lurched thinking of the years no one had remembered his special day.

He might be big and strong and self-sufficient, but he could use some tender loving care. And she was just the person to give it to him. Give him all the care she could to make up for the lonely years.

That was what was missing from this home. A woman's touch. Her eyes met his and she smiled.

When his gaze dropped to roam over her dress thoughtfully, she felt a *frisson* of excitement. To hide her reaction, she began to slice the cake.

"That's why you're dressed up," he murmured softly as he reached for the first gift.

He opened the presents from Grandfather first. A dark blue work shirt, a set of handkerchiefs from George and a picture album from Kerry were soon stacked beside his plate.

Then he took the present from Rennie. Lingering a moment as he studied its silver paper and white ribbon, he then tore it open and looked into the box. Nestled on cotton was a large silver belt buckle, engraved with a Texas longhorn.

"A little bit of Texas from me to you," Rennie said lightly when he continued to stare at it.

His smile warmed her to her toes as he looked up. Reaching out for her, he pulled her up from her chair and to his side, his arm easing around her waist, pulling her close to his chest.

"Thank you. You brought it with you?"

"Yes. Actually I brought it to be a wedding present, but when we didn't exchange gifts I saved it for your birthday. Good thing I saw it on the marriage license, huh?"

She smiled down at him, longing to brush back the lock of hair that had fallen across his brow. Her fingers almost tingled with the remembered feel of his hair. Then she became aware of the stricken silence.

She met his stunned eyes. Sudden realization of how bleak her wedding had been, of the lack of welcome to their family hit Hunter. Rennie could feel his regret as his gaze locked with hers.

"Dammit," Hunter muttered. "I should have bought you something. Women like things like that."

"Nonsense," she said, pushing aside the disappointment she'd felt when she'd known he wouldn't be giving her anything.

She'd expected something, and felt foolish when she'd realized that he never thought of their marriage beyond business. He hadn't even waited for her to change into the white dress she'd brought.

"It was foolishly romantic of me. We have a business arrangement, not a love-affair," she said, keeping the hurt from her voice.

She hadn't meant to spoil his birthday. She'd wanted the day to be special for him.

"Have some cake. Grandpa said it was your favorite," she said, trying to eradicate the tension. Hunter stared at her averted face, his own tight with anger and self-disgust. Finally, he accepted a piece of cake.

It was a somber dessert and Rennie could have kicked herself for spoiling the mood. She hadn't meant to. She'd only explained why she had the buckle. She didn't even know if he liked it.

"Never thought of it from your side before," George said after the silence had dragged on for long, tense moments. "You came a long way looking for something. Gave up your home and country for someone you'd never met."

She smiled.

"Isn't it nice it worked out?"

He opened his mouth as if to say it was still early days, but closed it without speaking and merely gave a curt nod.

Rennie could feel the tension emanating from Hunter as they ate cake and sipped coffee. The relaxed atmosphere from dinner vanished.

His gaze roamed over her as she ate, taking in the dainty lace, the pretty color the dress brought to her complexion. When everyone was finished eating, Hunter shoved back his chair and reached to take Rennie's arm, his warm fingers caressing her bare skin, sending tendrils of charged awareness shooting through her.

Rennie rose at his urging, her heart tripping in her chest.

"Grandpa, can you do the dishes tonight and see to Kerry? I want to talk to Rennie." Almost without waiting for his assent, Hunter pulled her around the table, scooped up her present and walked from the room. Instead of taking them outside, however, he headed for the hall, then the stairs.

In only seconds Hunter closed the door to his room behind them and spun her around, his expression unlike any Rennie had seen.

"Is something wrong?" she asked, unsure what he was doing.

"Not a thing," he replied, drawing her up against him, tossing her gift lightly at the end of the bed. "Only I'm not waiting until tomorrow night for you to share my room. I want you to start tonight."

With that he lowered his head and claimed her lips.

Her heart stuttered in her chest at his words and the heat that was so fiery began glowing within her at his touch. His mouth opened hers and delved into the sweetness within.

It was too soon. She wasn't ready.

Yet as the heady intoxication of his kiss swept through her she forgot to protest. Her body leaped in response to his embrace, craved his caresses, yearned to be wholly his. She relaxed against him, snuggling to get closer, her hands kneading the strong muscles of his shoulders, seeking to give him some means of pleasure to match the degree he ignited in her.

He raised his head, gazing down at her with heated eyes. Slowly his hands released the clips in her hair. Threading his fingers through her soft waves, he watched as his fingers explored the silken texture. His breathing was hard and fast, and his body pressed against hers, backing her against the solid door, though Rennie wondered who was pressing against whom.

He lowered his face again, raining soft kisses across her brow, her eyes, her cheeks. Teasing the corners of her mouth until she was whimpering with desire, Hunter quickly brought her mouth beneath his and plunged into the heat that welcomed him.

Rennie's desire raged beyond control as he brought her to a level of passion previously unknown. She'd never craved anything as much as she craved his touch. His exploration brought her to life, fiery, heated, surging life. She was lost to all around her save the man who held her.

Moving against him, she was inflamed. His lips captured hers, his tongue met hers, danced in the age-old ritual of passion. Her own hands learned the strength of his shoulders, the heat of his skin, the thickness of his hair, enraptured by the sensual wonder that Hunter generated.

When his hands began long, slow strokes down her side, she was floating on a sea of sensation, hot and arousing and incomplete. Her hands fumbled instinctively with the buttons of his shirt, slipping between them, feeling the smoldering heat of his skin, the steely strength of his muscles. Sliding across that expanse, she wanted to feel him against her, to absorb him.

Slowly the buttons yielded and his shirt parted. Greedily she pushed against him, reveling in the sensations of her feverish skin against his, her sensitized breasts further tantalized by the crisp curls on his chest, the warm steel of his muscles.

She was almost gasping for breath, but couldn't retreat an inch lest she loose the lifeline held by Hunter.

He slid her dress off her shoulders, over her hips, his hands lingering on her softly rounded bottom. The groan he gave at her touch filled her with a heady sense of power and she smiled against his mouth, knowing she could please him as he was pleasing her. He drew in a sharp breath.

Quickly he divested himself of his clothes and the

remainder of hers and lifted her on to the bed. In a split-second he came down on top of her and began slow kisses.

Rennie arched into him, her hands moving across his skin, her heart pounding, heated blood rushing through her veins.

The outside world had disappeared; there was only her and Hunter in a world of two. A hot, sensuous, sensory world where touch and heat and exquisite pleasure were the only realities.

An endless world where ecstasy was the summit.

Then Rennie was drifting on a cloud, pleasure satiated, delight remembered, floating on a tide of enchantment.

"Are you all right?"

Hunter's voice sounded softly in her ear, as he pulled her closer to his side, his body hot and damp against her.

"Mmm," she mumbled.

To talk would take more effort than she was capable of. If only time could cease and she could float forever on the bliss they'd shared.

"Thank you for my birthday cake and the present," he said, kissing her. "No one has ever done that for me before."

"Is this your way of saying thank you?" she said with an involuntary smile of sheer delight at his kisses.

She felt boneless, mindless, floaty.

"No, I think I consider this another birthday present."

He kissed the dimple on her cheek, moved to find her mouth. Kissing her slowly, gently, his lips moved against hers, but he didn't deepen the kiss.

"Mmm, nice," she said when he trailed kisses across her ear. "I think I like being married."

"It's a good thing, because as of now we are irrevocably married."

Rennie nodded, too tired to respond.

She wanted desperately to stay awake and impress every moment on her memory. She never wanted to forget this night. How astonishing that she had thought it too soon. It was just right. It had been the most glorious experience of her life and she didn't want to forget a second.

She relished the feel of Hunter against her, marveled at the passion he'd brought from her, savored the touch and taste of her husband, the shockingly masculine presence even now intimately aligned with her.

But she couldn't stay awake. She was spent. Still cocooned in the warm delight of his lovemaking, she drifted to sleep.

Rennie woke once during the night confused by the unexpected presence of another. Her head was pillowed on Hunter's uninjured shoulder, one arm across his chest. Her legs were tangled with his. He'd pulled a sheet over them, and his bare body kept her toasty warm.

Smiling gently with unexpected elation, Rennie closed her eyes and drifted back to sleep.

In the morning, she was alone. She woke slowly, realizing almost instantly that Hunter was gone. Rising up on one elbow, she glanced around. His boots were gone–he must have dressed and left. A glance at the clock showed it was still early. She needed to get up and dressed to get breakfast for the men.

Kerry was still asleep. Rennie hoped she'd stay asleep until the men left. Hurrying into the kitchen, she stopped short as two pairs of eyes turned to her. Color stained her cheeks as embarrassment flooded through her. She hadn't realized how awkward she'd feel to walk into the room where all present knew exactly what she and Hunter had been doing last night.

George's eyes didn't waver, and his expression gave nothing away. Almost stumbling, Rennie moved to the refrigerator to get the eggs. Hunter met her there, taking her hand in his and kissing the palm.

"Did you sleep all right?" he asked, releasing her and reaching for the bacon. She noted he'd worn the buckle she'd given him. Her heart lifted.

"Yes."

Avoiding his eyes, shyly remembering in broad daylight all that they'd done, she moved to the stove. She needed the routine of preparing breakfast to regain her assurance.

She was glad when the meal was finished and the men were ready to leave. By this afternoon she'd have herself in hand. Married people made love all the time. It was nothing to be shy about, she told herself.

Hunter paused at the door.

"I'll be back around noon to head into town to fetch Daphne. We'll be back here around three."

"Will you want lunch?"

"Just a sandwich to eat on the way."

He hesitated as if to say something else, but then stepped outside. She nodded, listening for Kerry, wondering if they could ride in with him.

When the baby was up, dressed and fed, it didn't take Rennie long to move her things from her room to Hunter's. She found space in the large closet for her dresses. Fingering his shirts and pants, she closed her eyes, drinking in his scent that lingered. When she put her frilly underwear in with his sturdy cotton briefs, she smiled, wondering what he'd think when he went to get dressed tomorrow.

She changed her sheets, dusted and swept and opened the windows for a breeze. The room looked nice. Daphne would have nothing to complain about.

To her disappointment Hunter didn't invite her to go with him to get Daphne. Rennie stood on the front veranda watching as he drove away. She wished she didn't have this nagging worry about Daphne Adams.

Rennie was sitting in the new rocking chair on the veranda when Hunter returned. Kerry was playing near by with her dolly and looked up when she heard the car. She scurried over to Rennie and leaned against her knee as she watched the car approach.

Rennie brushed her hair back from her face and smiled at her. Kerry's green and white sun suit was not as crisp as when she'd first put it on, but the dust would brush off. Her hair had grown slightly and Rennie had trimmed it so that it didn't look so much like a boy's. Her heart warmed as she took in how precious Kerry was.

Wouldn't her aunt love her to bits?

Taking Kerry's finger out of her mouth, Rennie squeezed her hand lightly and stood up as the car stopped before the veranda.

The woman emerging from the station wagon was tall and willowy. Her white pants molded her perfect figure as if they had been painted on. Her loose vibrant blue top hung off one shoulder, exposing her creamy skin. Her short blond hair was cut in the latest style and her make-up highlighted her best features, her dark brown eyes.

Rennie could tell by the way she clung to Hunter's hand when he assisted her from the car, the way she smiled up at him and angled her eyes just so that Daphne was on the make.

Hunter made introductions, not appearing to be aware of Daphne's clinging hand.

"I couldn't believe it when Hunter told me he was married. It came as such a shock."

An unpleasant one, if her expression was anything to go by. Her eyes told Rennie that she couldn't believe it was to someone like her.

Rennie merely smiled and nodded, leading Kerry toward her aunt.

"And here's Kerry. How long has it been since you've seen her?"

"Not since before Tessa died."

Daphne smiled at Kerry, looking like a fashion plate.

"Hello, little niece."

When Kerry smiled shyly and toddled over to be picked up, Daphne stepped back hastily.

"No, no, honey, mustn't touch Auntie's pants."

She looked up at Rennie.

"I'll wait until she's cleaned up before holding her. She's all dirty."

Turning to Hunter, Daphne smiled.

"I can't wait for you to show me all round the station. Tessa talked so much about it. I'm dying to see everything!"

"I don't think white is the best color to wear around here," he said evenly as he watched Rennie pick up Kerry.

Her own blue shorts and stripped cotton shirt would stand a little dust, Rennie thought as she hugged Kerry close, knowing the baby was too young to be hurt by her aunt's snippy rejection, but angry herself on Kerry's behalf.

"I did bring some other clothes. Even some jeans. I'm sure I'll fit right in," Daphne declared happily.

Rennie hadn't expected to like Daphne and she didn't. Though she hadn't expected the shaft of jealousy that pierced her at the sight of Daphne smiling up at Hunter and him smiling back. She watched as they drew the luggage from the car.

Daphne chatted artlessly with Hunter as she took a small bag and he drew out two larger ones. How long was she planning to stay? And where was her supposed devotion to her niece? She seemed a lot more intent on Hunter than Kerry.

She remembered that George had said they'd dated around the time that Alex and Tessa had married. How far had their relationship gone? Had he kissed her? Kissed Daphne the way he'd kissed her last night? Had he made love to her?

Her heart contracted and she felt a wave of desolation sweep through her. She hoped not. She couldn't bear the thought.

"What a beautiful room," Daphne said as Hunter placed her cases beside the dresser. Rennie had followed them up the stairs with the intent of bathing Kerry so that she'd be clean enough to suit her aunt. She hesitated in the doorway and watched as Daphne examined everything in the room.

"It's just perfect! Thank you, Hunter," she added, her voice dropping to an intimate level as she smiled up at him.

"Thank Rennie, she decorated it. She's redoing the whole house."

He missed the flash of anger in her eyes when Daphne heard it was Rennie who had decorated the room.

"If you need anything, just call."

"I'm sure Rennie has thought of everything. If not, I'll be sure to ask her."

Though the words were innocuous, the tone was definitely not. Rennie moved away before she was tempted to answer the unspoken challenge.

After bathing Kerry and dressing her in a fresh sun suit to make certain that the baby would meet Daphne's exacting standards, Rennie knocked on her bedroom door. There was no answer. Puzzled, Rennie took Kerry downstairs.

She heard voices on the veranda and pushed through the screen door. Daphne was holding court. There was no other way to describe it, Rennie thought. Daphne was sitting in her new rocking chair. George and Hunter sat on either side, laughing easily at something she had just said. Of course, they'd all known each other for years. For a moment, Rennie felt an outsider again, like a guest who was reluctantly tolerated.

"There's my precious niece. Come to Auntie, darling," Daphne said when she spotted Rennie holding Kerry. "I've brought you a lovely doll and a book to read."

Her smile was charming, and she eagerly reached for the little girl, settling her on her lap, rocking her slowly. "I can't believe how much she's grown, and how good she looks," she said as she smiled at Hunter.

Hunter tilted back his chair, watching Daphne with narrowed eyes. He smiled slightly when she said Kerry looked good.

"You should have seen her before Rennie arrived and took her in hand. She looked like a ragamuffin."

Ignoring Rennie, still standing on the periphery of the group, Daphne lowered her voice again.

"I should have come sooner. I didn't realize how hard it would be for you. I could have taken Kerry in hand. She's my niece too, after all, Hunter. We should have shared the burden."

She spoke only to Hunter.

"You had your work in Sydney. She's fine here," Hunter replied.

"Pull up a chair," George said when Rennie remained standing.

Hunter didn't even glance around.

As if he'd released her from a spell, she shook her head.

"No, thanks, I need to get dinner started."

She turned and headed for the kitchen, anger and jealousy building.

Just who did Daphne think she was, sashaying in and making a play for her husband? Hunter was hers and the sooner Daphne realized it the better. And what was he doing paying any attention to her? Didn't he remember he had a wife who loved him?

Rennie stopped dead, shocked at the thought. Oh, good grief, that was impossible. She couldn't love Hunter. She hadn't meant to fall in love ever.

But she couldn't help herself. If she thought about it, he was all she had wanted her entire life. Strong, reliant, caring, sexy. She considered a moment longer. Bossy, arrogant and demanding were not traits she'd longed for. But they all added up to make him who he was.

She smiled in wonder. Would Daphne's visit threaten

that? Would Hunter come to believe that an Australian woman was more his taste? That Kerry's aunt was a better choice for Kerry's mother than a stranger from America?

Hurt and jealousy warred within her as she slowly resumed walking to the kitchen. She might be a tiny bit in love with him, but she dared not tell him. Not unless he somehow showed her that he regarded her as more than a business partner.

It'd be too awkward and embarrassing to admit to the feelings that had sprung up in their business arrangement.

He'd never asked for something like that. He'd warned her against it! And, after all her fine talk scoffing love, she dared not be the one to bring it up.

As Rennie prepared for bed that night she wondered how she'd be able to deal with Daphne for the next five days. If this afternoon had been an example, Rennie would go stark staring insane before Daphne left. The visit stretched out endlessly.

Rennie remembered each word at dinner as if it had been recorded. The woman was annoying, but could be entertaining. She'd been caustic and cynical when describing certain aspects of her life in Sydney, yet amusing and interesting.

She seemed genuinely interested in Kerry's progress, yet didn't want to hold her or spend much time with her.

But Rennie was most upset about what she considered to be Daphne's play for Hunter. It didn't help to know that she was jealous of the woman and uncertain because of her own tenuous relationship with her new husband.

"I can't wait to see over the station, Hunter," Daphne had

said. "Can we start right after dinner? I'm here for such a short time and don't want to miss a thing."

"What about Kerry? I thought you came to see her?" Rennie had blurted out before Hunter could answer, uneasy with the thought of his showing Daphne everything.

Rennie hadn't been fully shown over the homestead, much less the entire station. Shouldn't Hunter show her first?

"Doesn't she go to bed soon? Now would be the perfect time to explore. That way I can spend lots of time with her tomorrow when she's awake."

Daphne's friendly response had sounded logical, but it irritated Rennie.

"We can see some of the homestead after dinner, before it gets too dark. Rennie can take care of the baby," Hunter had said, frowning at Rennie as if displeased by her comment.

Her heart dropped. Their only private time was after dinner. Of course she'd known that they couldn't disappear and leave their guest, but it hurt that he'd forsake their time entirely to spend it with Daphne.

Dusk had turned to darkness now and they were still gone. Rennie had sat on the veranda with George after putting Kerry down, both silent with their own thoughts. Rennie tried hard to refrain from counting the minutes Hunter spent with Daphne. But the evening dragged on.

And they still weren't back.

7

Rennie climbed into the large bed, memories of last night crowding in. Switching off the light, she wondered where her husband was and what he was doing. Somehow she'd thought that after spending a night together their relationship would be on a different footing now, a stronger one.

But he seemed to hold himself apart today.

How could he compartmentalize everything? Hadn't last night meant anything to him?

A shaft of light from the hall spilled into the room when Hunter opened the door a little later. He hesitated a moment, then closed it behind him and crossed the darkened room to the bed.

"Rennie?" His voice was quiet.

"I'm awake if you want to turn on the light," she said softly, hiding her anger, relieved that he'd returned at last.

She refused to look at the clock; she didn't want to know how late it was.

"I'll use the bathroom."

She heard him prepare for bed, then felt the mattress shift as he lifted the sheet and slid in beside her. Rennie willed herself to remain still, to ignore the intense longing that filled her to fling herself across the small distance that separated them and throw herself against his hard body.

Hunter obviously had no such compunctions and in only seconds his strong arms reached out and drew her up against the length of him. For a brief moment she began to relax.

Then she frowned.

"I can smell her perfume on you," she said coolly, pulling back.

What had they been doing the hours they were away? She suddenly felt hurt. He hadn't promised love, but had talked of fidelity.

Had it only been talk? Was he the same as Stuart? Was fidelity only to apply to her?

"Daphne is a snuggler. She clung to my arm the entire time, afraid of falling. She shouldn't have worn those strappy sandals. She couldn't keep her balance."

He sounded tired.

Rennie smiled sadly. How clever of Daphne. Maybe she should try it herself.

"You were gone a long time."

She couldn't resist saying it. She wanted to scream it, demand to know where they'd been, what they'd done. Remind him that he had married her two weeks ago and shouldn't be out with other women till all hours of the night.

"Lots to see. She's never been on a station before."

"Neither have I. You could have taken me around, too."

She could feel his head turn on the pillow as he stared at her.

"If you wanted to go, why not say so?"

"I was told to watch Kerry, remember? Besides, I wouldn't want to intrude where I wasn't wanted," she muttered.

"Don't go imagining things that aren't there," he snapped. "Now, you sound like Tessa."

"Did she have reasons to suspect Alex?" Rennie asked.

"Suspect him of what? For pity's sake, I showed a visitor around, she had a lot of questions. It took a while. You sound jealous."

"No," she denied quickly lest he think about it more.

"Go to sleep." He softened the command when he added, "I'm tired and there's a lot to do tomorrow."

Rennie waited a moment, but he said nothing further, nor made any move to kiss her goodnight. He'd probably had all the kisses he needed that night from Daphne.

Slowly Rennie pulled away, disappointed that Hunter made no move to hold her. She felt cold and alone in the big bed as she clung to her side. Sleep proved elusive and she had only her own tormented thoughts to keep her company.

* * *

"Are you in trouble with the law?" Daphne asked the next afternoon when she and Rennie were sitting on the veranda.

Kerry was sleeping and the two women had been drawn to the coolness of the covered porch. Talk was desultory, as if both knew they had nothing in common, yet had to put up with each other.

Rennie looked up as the official car drew to a stop before the house. She smiled when she recognized Gerry Dalton's lanky frame as he climbed out.

Then she remembered Hunter's admonition to stay away from Gerry. But she could hardly run into the house and slam the door in his face when he'd come to call. Besides, wasn't he a friend of Hunter's?

"Hello."

She stood and crossed to the shallow steps to greet him.

Daphne remained sitting, watching the exchange with avid eyes.

"I thought I'd drop by and see how you were adjusting to life on the outback."

He handed her a bouquet of pink roses, some still buds, others already opening, spilling their heady fragrance into the afternoon air.

"How lovely. Thank you. I love roses–they're my favorite flower. I'm hoping to plant some around here when I get the house fixed up. Come up. We were just enjoying the shade. Would you like some iced tea or lemonade?"

"Lemonade."

He was almost as big as Hunter and filled the space near her. Rennie introduced him to Daphne and left to put the bouquet into water and fetch another glass of lemonade.

When she rejoined the two on the veranda they were chatting casually together. Rennie sat before Daphne smiled maliciously at Gerry.

"I just realized why your name was so familiar. You were a special friend of my sister, Tessa, weren't you?"

He looked up at her, startled.

"I didn't realize you were Tessa's sister."

He didn't confirm or deny the statement.

"No reason you should. Come to visit with Hunter's wife now?"

Audaciously she watched Gerry, her gaze flickering to Rennie.

"Just a friendly call," he said, his eyes narrowed as he surveyed Daphne.

"How neighborly. She's new in Australia, you know. Doesn't have many friends."

"I know that. She'll meet others in time."

Rennie knew there was something she was missing, she could feel the undercurrents to the conversation, but she was at a loss to understand exactly what it was.

In the back of her mind were Hunter's words to stay away from Gerry, but he seemed harmless, friendly. Surely visiting him on the veranda with Daphne wouldn't cause a problem.

"You haven't been into town recently, have you?" Gerry turned to Rennie with an easy smile.

"No, there's so much to do around here. I only went in one day to get some things," she said, glad that the conversation was becoming general.

"Doing up the place, I hear," Gerry said.

Rennie wondered where he'd heard.

"A little. It seems like years since anyone has done anything to fix it up."

Rennie turned to Daphne. "I was surprised to find that Tessa hadn't done much."

The other woman shrugged.

"She was after Alex to build them their own place. She felt like an outsider here and didn't want to waste her time decorating when she planned to move soon."

"She wasn't happy on the station," Gerry said gently.

"No, she was a city girl. It was too bad she fell for Alex," Daphne said, with another elegant shrug. "But the money was good and I'm sure that was part of the attraction."

"Money?" Rennie repeated, puzzled.

Daphne's brown eyes narrowed as she studied Rennie.

"Don't try to tell me you didn't know how wealthy the Bradshaw's are. Besides this station, they have interest in gold mines, opal mines, plus shipping. Though you wouldn't think it from this place. It sure needs some work."

"From what I can tell, except for Tessa's brief sojourn here, there hasn't been a woman living here for thirty years. No wonder it isn't exactly a showplace. And no, I didn't know anything about money."

Rennie felt a spurt of anger again.

Hadn't Hunter trusted her enough to let her know there was more to his life than the station? How dared George say that she threatened bankruptcy if she spent anything in town? She'd been feeling badly about that since that day.

Now, if Daphne was to be believed, the paltry amount she spent wouldn't even be noticed. And why would he have needed Marjorie's money?

"Well, maybe the money's plowed back into the station. It sure isn't spent on furniture or clothes," Daphne said disdainfully.

Rennie looked away. Maybe Hunter was strapped for cash and had seen the perfect opportunity to obtain a much needed influx by marrying her. Had he lied about the real reasons for their marriage? Was Kerry only the excuse? Was the true reason need for the money?

Just then Kerry called from her room, awake from her nap. As Rennie rose, Daphne put her glass on the table.

"I'll see to her, you visit with your friend," the blond woman said, jumping up and hurrying to the door.

"I didn't expect to see any of Tessa's family on Silver Creek Station. Heard in town that Hunter's trying for custody of Kerry. Why's she here?" Gerry asked as the screen slammed behind her.

"To visit Kerry. Hunter was worried she'd come over the custody issue. Her parents want to raise Kerry, you know. But so far she hasn't mentioned anything about it."

"She's not like her sister," he said musingly.

"What was Tessa like?" Rennie asked. "I haven't seen any pictures. I hope her parents have some so Kerry can see what her mother looked like when she's older."

"Tessa was small with light hair and brown eyes similar to Daphne's. Only Tessa wasn't strong, like Daphne appears. She had romantic notions a mile wide of marriage and life on the outback. The reality was too harsh for her." Gerry's tone was tender, his thoughts far away.

"So she left," Rennie said.

"She tried to talk Alex into moving to Sydney, or even Darwin, but he was too stubborn. He wanted to stay at Silver Creek."

"His work was here. She knew that when they were married," Rennie said.

Had Tessa married thinking to change her new husband? Even Rennie knew that a woman couldn't change a man.

Gerry nodded, his expression clearing.

"But I didn't come here to talk about people you don't know and never will. Next time you come to town, we'll have coffee and I'll introduce you around."

"I'll probably be in next week."

Though Hunter should be the one introducing her

around. She'd wait until he could accompany her.

Wanting to change the subject, Rennie said, "Once Daphne leaves, I want to continue decorating the house, and then plant a garden. Where did you get the roses?"

"Mamie Jordan grows them. She has a house in town and the largest garden around."

"And you talked her out of some roses?"

"Told her they were for a beautiful woman not yet used to the bleakness of the outback."

Rennie was uneasy with his facile compliment. She was a married woman–should he be talking to her like that?

"They're lovely. I'm glad to know they grow out here. I wasn't sure. But you were wrong," she said gently. "I don't find the outback bleak. It's got a haunting beauty of its own."

"I'm used to it, but a trip to Darwin comes in handy to break the monotony. It's green up on top, tropical."

"I'll have to go sometime," she muttered, thinking of all the different places she'd like to visit in Australia.

Did Hunter take vacations? Did he like to travel?

"Well, duty calls. I must be on my way. Remember to look me up when you come to Boolong Creek next time," Gerry said as he stood and reached out his hand to draw Rennie up.

He held her hand a shade longer than was necessary, then released it, smiling ruefully.

Rennie watched him uneasily as he drove off, wondering why he'd come. She was sure there was more than merely wanting to say hello. It was over an hour's drive from town.

Had he heard that Daphne was visiting and wanted to meet her? Had he hoped Hunter would be around? No, he hadn't even asked after his friend. Gathering the empty glasses, Rennie went to begin dinner.

"How did you and Kerry get along today?" Hunter asked Daphne that evening as soon as they were seated around the large dining-room table. Rennie had refused to serve dinner in the kitchen when they had a guest.

"She was an angel. We spent a lot of time together today, didn't we, sweetie?" Daphne smiled at her niece, then at Hunter, her eyes wide and guileless. "And I'm sure Rennie was glad I was here to watch her this afternoon when her visitor called. So nice not to have the bother of a baby when entertaining."

Hunter turned to look at his wife.

"You had a visitor? Who?"

"More of a close friend, I thought," Daphne murmured before Rennie could reply.

Hunter's expression grew darker.

"I wasn't aware you'd had the chance to make any friends here. Who was it?" he asked again, his expression curious as he waited for Rennie's reply.

"Gerry Dalton stopped by," she said, meeting his gaze.

She could see the anger flare. She could clearly hear the echo of his admonition to stay away from Gerry.

"I told you to stay away from him," Hunter bit out, his eyes impaling her.

"Oh, Rennie, I'm sorry. I didn't realize I shouldn't have said anything. Though maybe you shouldn't have set his roses on the table," Daphne said prettily, looking contrite and sly at the same time.

Hunter glared at the flowers, then at Rennie, his lips tightening as his eyes darkened. His anger was evident.

"I know you said to stay away from him, but he just

showed up. What was I to do, slam the door in his face? He said he was a friend of yours," Rennie defended herself.

She could feel all eyes on her and knew the two men of the family thought she was in the wrong, but she didn't know why.

"He was once, but isn't any longer. Dammit, I don't have to give you a reason for doing something—I'm boss of this operation and you follow orders. I don't expect to have to repeat myself. Once should be enough for you. Is that clear?" he ground out, his eyes like hardened steel.

Rennie stared at him in disbelief. She couldn't believe that he'd order her around as if she were a stock man, couldn't believe that he'd chastise her before everyone.

Remembering when he'd told her to stay away from Gerry, she recalled that Kerry had been stung and interrupted them. Had he not been planning to tell her then why she should stay away? Was she just to do his bidding in everything without knowing why?

Before she could protest, however, Daphne spoke again.

"Oh, dear, Gerry Dalton. Hunter, I just remembered where I heard the name. Wasn't he the man who Tessa ran off with?"

The silence was thundering. Rennie swung around to stare at Daphne in stunned horror. All wide-eyed innocence, Daphne gazed fixedly at Hunter. Slowly Rennie scanned the other faces, anger and resentment showing in George's. When her eyes met Hunter's again, she shivered at the condemnation evident in his expression.

"I'm sorry. I didn't know. I won't speak to him again," she whispered, stunned at the anger she saw in Hunter's eyes.

Hope died in her breast at his look. There was nothing of love or commitment in his gaze.

She felt as if she'd been judged and found wanting.

Conversation gradually resumed around the table, but Rennie was excluded. She kept her eyes on her plate and finished her dinner in silence.

What was she doing here? She had no business getting tangled up in a family she didn't know because she'd wanted one of her own for so long. It wasn't just that, however. It had also been because of the money needed to aid her grandmother. That hadn't changed.

"I'd love to give Kerry her bath tonight," Daphne said when they'd finished eating. "Show me where everything is, Hunter?" she asked as she lifted the little girl and kissed her cheek. "I don't have a lot of time to visit and want to see her as much as possible," she said, ignoring Rennie.

Tears burned in Rennie's eyes and her throat ached as she cleared the table and began to wash the dishes. Everyone had escaped the dining-room in record haste, leaving her alone with the clean-up.

It had been an honest mistake—she hadn't known the history of Gerry and Tessa. But she knew Daphne had known from day one. Her set-up at dinner hadn't fooled Rennie.

But it didn't matter—it had fooled Hunter. The damage was done. George hadn't accepted her from the first. Was Hunter now regretting their hasty marriage?

How dare he show his anger in front of the others. And his do as I say because I'm in charge rankled. She wasn't some employee to be ordered around.

She felt like an outcast. Maybe marriage by agreement

wasn't enough. Maybe there had to be at least an affectionate relationship first to insure that the union would endure.

She'd been here for over two weeks, doing the best she could to cook and clean and make the house a home. Yet in only two days Daphne had come in and disrupted all her progress.

And Hunter had let her.

Her anger grew.

When she'd finished the dishes, Rennie slipped out the back door and wandered down to the horse barn. Once inside, she dragged a bale of hay against the wall and leaned back, watching the horses munch their feed, their glances curious.

Tears threatened as she remembered the scene at dinner and she closed her eyes, willing them away. But to no avail. They slipped down her cheeks, and for a few moments she gave herself the luxury of crying.

Had she made a mistake coming to Australia? She was homesick. She was in a strange place. She hadn't even spoken with her grandmother–only exchanged emails.

She brushed her cheeks and tried to think. She couldn't let Daphne ruin things. She still wanted to be married, to raise Kerry, to live with Hunter, maybe even have children of her own in the future. But did he still want that?

And what could she do to make it all work?

She wished she could talk with Gram. But she was in the hospital now, getting the treatment needed for her recovery.

Rennie missed her. She'd never felt so alone.

Hunter found her there half an hour later, listlessly playing with a wisp of hay.

"Rennie?"

She looked up and watched as his long legs brought him swiftly across to stand beside her. Her heart caught in her chest and she pressed her hand to the spot to ease the ache she felt when she saw him.

"I'm sorry I spoke to Gerry after you said for me not to," she said, "but the reason would have helped. And I didn't invite him here. Was I to be totally rude? Is that how things are done in Australia?"

He towered over her as she sat on the bale of hay. As if he realized it, he hunkered down so that his face was level with hers.

"I'm sorry I yelled at you in front of everyone. It wasn't right. I apologize."

She shrugged, dragging her eyes away from his silvery gaze.

He reached for her left hand and took it gently in his, his finger and thumb twisting the shiny new wedding-ring round and round on her finger.

"Tessa was unhappy here on the station. She went into Boolong Creek as often as she could, which was almost every day. We knew she wanted more from life than keeping house on the station, but Alex loved ranching and didn't want to move to a city. He was planning to build her a house and thought maybe that would make her happy. I should have explained things to you."

Rennie watched his hand twisting her ring, his touch doing strange and wonderful things to her emotions.

She wished she were confident enough to ruffle her fingers through his thick hair, touch the hard plane of his cheek, trace the firm line of his lips. Instead she concentrated on what he was saying, trying to understand.

"Anyway, one day she left. Gerry had come for her and taken her to Darwin. From there she'd flown to Sydney."

"Was she going off with Gerry?" Rennie asked. "Or was he merely her transportation away from here?"

Hunter looked up at that, puzzled.

"She was running off with him, of course."

"So what do you expect now, that I'll run off with him?" she asked.

He stared into her eyes for a long time, silent as if searching for the truth of the situation, seeking to learn her secrets.

"Maybe."

His hand tightened on hers, squeezing her fingers hard.

"I know there's no love between us and we both knew that going into this marriage. But I sure as hell don't want to find you falling for someone else. You knew the terms before you even left Texas. I expect loyalty and integrity from my wife."

"But not love?" she whispered, her heart breaking slightly at his harsh words.

She longed for love from her handsome husband, longed to lavish on him the affection she felt growing for him.

"No, I don't expect love. That wasn't part of the deal."

"Why did you marry me?"

"Why the question now? I told you at the beginning, I wanted a mother for Kerry."

"Not for the money?"

She looked up at him, trying to gauge his response. Would he tell her the truth now that it didn't matter?

"If I married you for the money would it make your own

motive seem more pure? Look around you, this is a prosperous station. Do I look as if I need money?"

"My motives were never in question. You knew from the beginning that I needed the money for Gram's medical care."

"We both benefited from this arrangement," he bit out, his eyes stormy.

"One more than the other, perhaps."

Her own anger was rising.

"What do you mean by that?" he asked silkily.

"Just that I gave up everything to come here. Even the money doesn't do me much good beyond helping my grandmother. Where can I spend it here?"

"It's too late to be having second thoughts. You knew what to expect before you came."

His voice was hard, flat.

"There won't be wild parties, trips to Sydney or Darwin, and no carrying on with other men. That was our agreement."

"And no carrying on with other women," she shot back.

"I have no need for that. I have a wife to provide that outlet."

Hope died within her and she sagged in defeat.

So much for her wish that he'd love her one day. He'd made it plain that he had no time for such foolishness. And the insulting comment he'd just made proved the point.

She had no one to blame but herself for holding out such an absurd hope.

She tugged at her hand, aching from his grip, as her heart was aching from his harsh words. An outlet. Was that all she was?

"I don't feel anything for Gerry Dalton, nor expect to,

ever. I wouldn't run off from you, Hunter. We're married and I'll abide by my vows," she said firmly.

He released her and stood towering over her, his expression still angry. Then, reaching down, he grasped her arm and gently lifted her to her feet.

"Come back to the house now. We have a guest to entertain."

Rennie was asleep when Hunter came to bed, but he woke her and deliberately made love to her. He never said a word, but she cried out her growing love for him in her heart wondering if she'd ever say it aloud, wondering if he'd ever feel anything for her beyond the fact that she was convenient.

When they were finished, she lay with her head on his shoulder, her arm across his chest, his strong legs tangled with hers. She was still flushed and hot, and his body was warm. Slowly she traced the muscles of his chest, feeling their shape, the iron hardness that had come from the constant work around the station, feeling the strong beat of his heart.

Life was unexpected. She wondered if this was how her mother had felt each time she'd fancied herself in love.

How had she stood the rejection when the men left?

Rennie's feelings were bittersweet.

She loved this man, yet had to acknowledge that he might never care for her or see her as anything beyond a means to provide Kerry with a mother.

Would it have been better if she hadn't come to Australia?

He captured her wandering hand and brought her wrist to his mouth, kissing her softly, his lips warm and damp. Tracing up to her palm, he kissed it with his open mouth, sweeping the softness of her skin with his tongue.

Rennie felt his erotic touch to her toes. She was already warm and languid from his lovemaking, and yet his touch reignited the spiraling heat within her.

She tilted her head to see him, but it was too dark. The faint light from the stars and moon enabled her to see his silhouette only. She wished she could see his expression. Was it loving?

Or was she just a convenient outlet for his sexual desires? The outlet that would keep him from straying?

He returned her hand to his chest, holding it loosely, his thumb brushing back and forth across the back of her fingers.

"Rennie, has Daphne said anything to you about Kerry?"

"Beyond the day-to-day questions about her activities, no. Why, are you worried about the custody issue?"

"Yes. She asked me about it the first night. She was surprised to learn I had married. When I told her we married to provide a stable environment for Kerry, she seemed satisfied. She hasn't brought it up again, but she makes me uneasy."

Rennie's heart sank. So Daphne knew that theirs was a business arrangement, not a real marriage. Even if Hunter hadn't told her in so many words, Daphne would have gleaned that from the manner in which she was treated—not as a cherished wife, but more like an employee.

"It's important that she understand that Kerry will have a stable, loving home. That's why I was so angry about Gerry. I don't want her to think anything would jeopardize Kerry's stability. I don't want Kerry raised in Sydney. She's Alex's daughter. I want her to know his home."

"I understand," Rennie said softly.

Suddenly curious, she tried again to see him in the dark.

"Is that why we're making love—to make this seem as normal a marriage as possible, to show Daphne?"

She almost held her breath as she waited for his reply.

He rose upon one elbow, leaning over her as if to see her in the dark.

"I would hardly discuss this with Daphne," he said.

His hand rested on her shoulder, his thumb brushing her smooth, supple skin.

"Then why?" she whispered.

"We're married, tied in a bond of mutual support. It's a natural human characteristic to mate male with female. And you're very female, sweetheart. Very desirable."

His hand moved to her throat, his thumb leaving a trail of fiery excitement as it skimmed against her jaw.

"A natural human characteristic."

She was crushed. At every turn Hunter reaffirmed their business arrangement. She couldn't speak for fear that her disappointment would spill out.

"But the situation between you and Gerry needs to be made clear to Daphne. I sure as hell don't want her taking anything back to her parents that might suggest we don't have a strong bond. That would give fodder to a court delay," he continued, oblivious to her distress.

"There's no situation between me and Gerry," she said.

Tears welled, and she blinked, desperately trying to stem them before they spilled. She couldn't tell him why she was crying. He'd never understand.

"What do I do if Gerry comes again?" she whispered, wishing she dared use her fingers to brush the tears from her eyelids.

But Hunter continued to caress her throat, feeding the growing sensuality in her.

"I'll deal with Gerry. He won't be coming again."

"And Daphne?"

"I'll take care of her, too. She won't be here much longer."

"I don't think she believes our marriage is real," she murmured.

"She will before she leaves."

Rennie drifted to sleep, her heart hollow with the longing for more from Hunter. Would he ever come to care for her?

8

When Rennie awoke the next morning, the bed was empty. She stretched slowly and rolled over, noting that the bathroom door was shut. He hadn't left yet. She glanced at the clock. Plenty of time for breakfast, she'd get up after he left. Lying back down, she watched the closed door, waiting.

Hunter came from the bathroom dressed for the day in a faded red shirt and well-worn blue jeans, the Texas longhorn buckle hugging his lean belly. He looked virile and strong in his daily attire, and Rennie feasted her eyes on him, love swelling within her at the sight. His boots were clean, but they'd be dust-covered by day's end, as would his clothes.

But the dust couldn't hide the potency of him even then, and now, freshly showered and shaved, he was fantastic. She let her gaze trail over him. The bruise on his jaw had faded. He had left off the bulky bandage and the muscles of his arms showed smooth and sleek beneath the cotton of his shirt. Her heart raced as she felt the familiar pull of attraction, unable to tear her gaze away.

"Good morning, sleepyhead."

He came to the bed and sat on the edge, leaning over to kiss her warmly on her mouth.

"Wear jeans today. I'm taking you and Daphne around the station."

Rennie brightened.

"I'd like that. I've been dying to see more of it since I got here. Are we riding?"

She sat up, then blushed when she realized that she no longer wore her nightgown, and snatched the sheet up to her neck. Hunter chuckled at her reaction, leaning over to whisper in her ear.

"Not fair tempting me this early. We've things to do today. Get dressed."

Straightening, he moved toward the door.

"We'll take the truck. Hurry up so we can get breakfast behind us."

Rennie watched him leave and lay back down for a minute, depressed. He seemed effectively to dismiss their lovemaking once daylight arrived.

Of course in his eyes it was only mating; he didn't attach any special significance to it, while she gloried in it. For a little while she pretended that he loved her and that they would build a wonderful future together.

A little fantasy couldn't hurt. As long as she never forgot it was fantasy.

She hurriedly dressed, donning fresh jeans and a pretty blue top that enhanced the color in her eyes. Pulling her hair back into a ponytail, she soothed lotion on her face and touched up her eyelashes with mascara.

Satisfied that she looked the part of rancher's wife, she turned to face the day.

George had volunteered to watch Kerry, so when Hunter drew the Ute around to the back door Rennie left with a clear conscience, excited to see more of Silver Creek Station.

Daphne wore designer jeans and fancy tooled boots. Her yellow top was snug and low-cut, revealing more skin than Rennie thought appropriate. But she shrugged, determined not to let it bother her today. If Daphne got sun burnt, it'd be her own fault.

The truck was dusty but Rennie didn't care. She knew that by the end of the day they'd all probably be covered in a thin layer of the red dirt. Didn't Hunter look that way after a hard day?

She slanted him a quick glance as he watched her and Daphne climb in. As he patiently waited for them, his gaze met hers and he stared at her for a long moment, then his features softened slightly and he patted the bench seat beside him.

"Scoot over, sweetheart, so Daphne has room."

Thrilled at the meaningless endearment despite herself, Rennie slid up against him, instantly aware of his attraction and sexual pull. His thighs were sprawled apart, his left one pressing against hers, the heat at contact almost scorching. The sleeves of his shirt were rolled back, exposing his tanned arms, his muscles relaxed as his hands rested on the wheel.

She wished he'd use the endearment when they were alone, and not just for show around Daphne.

When Daphne climbed in and slammed the door, she immediately rolled down the window.

"It's warm already. What's it going to be like later?" she asked, looking across Rennie to question Hunter.

"Hot," he said as he pulled away.

The ride was bouncy as the vehicle roared across the ground. Feeling jostled and tossed about, Rennie had nothing to hold on to. Daphne at least could grasp the door for some balance. As the truck rolled and twisted, Rennie was thrown again and again against Hunter.

"Sorry," she murmured for the tenth time as she came off the seat several inches and almost landed in his lap.

"Easy, Rennie," he said, one arm coming around her to pull her closer to him. "Hold on to me. I'll slow down some to minimize the bumps."

"Do you frequently use this around the station?" she asked, eyes darting here and there as she sought to see everything. There were no roads or tracks; he just drove over virgin ground.

Normally Hunter rode the big black stallion, Ace.

"If I need to carry any equipment. Otherwise I prefer riding horseback."

Daphne coughed and waved her hand in front of her face.

"Hunter, this dust is awful. Can you slow down?"

He complied.

"Roll up your window a little, that might help. If we go any slower we'll never get anywhere."

She complied, then fanned her hand again.

"Now it's getting hot. No wonder you look like you roll in the dust every day if this is what it's like."

She rolled the window down again and promptly began coughing.

"How about Rennie trades with me? Maybe the dust won't affect her as much," she suggested brightly.

Hunter slowed and stopped.

"We can try. All right, Rennie?"

She wanted to refuse, but politeness prevailed.

"I'll try it."

In only moments they resumed the journey with Daphne in the center seat. Rennie didn't find the dust that bad.

It only came up occasionally, and was far preferable to the heat in the cab with the window closed. And she was able to hold on to the door and keep her seat better.

Daphne had the problem of bouncing now. She quickly put a hand on Hunter's thigh to balance herself. Rennie saw the movement and wanted to snatch the woman's hand away and berate her for touching her husband.

But she said nothing, looking out the window at the landscape, soon spotting grazing cattle, trying to ignore their guest and her pushy ways, appalled at her burning jealousy.

She was doubly hurt when Hunter also made no protest.

"This is one of the bores I was telling you about, Rennie."

Hunter stopped near a small pool, muddy banks surrounding it. He got out of the car. Daphne quickly scrambled after him and hurried to join him as he waited in the front for Rennie. When she reached him, she looked around avidly. The water was clear and looked cool in the hot day. Cattle grazed near by, in easy reach of the water.

"It's really hot now."

Daphne made a production of pulling her top away from her body to circulate air.

Hunter turned away and glanced at Rennie. Without a word, he lifted his hat from his head and plopped it on hers, tilting it to shade her face. When she turned startled eyes up at him, he smiled.

"Don't want you getting sunstroke."

"Do you have a hat for me?" Daphne said saucily, eyeing the one on Rennie.

"Sorry, didn't bring any extras. You aren't in as much danger with brown eyes. Blue-eyed blonds are very susceptible."

His response was offhand and he was already walking toward the pool.

Rennie almost exploded with giddiness at his concern. Refraining from throwing a triumphant grin at Daphne, she followed Hunter, her heart lighter than it had been in days.

"Tell me more about the water holes," she said.

Hunter explained how the artesian wells, once tapped, sent a continuous supply of water to the arid land, and how his grandfather, then he, had drilled different bores to expand their grazing area.

"And they never go dry?" she asked.

"No, the aquifer is huge. We count on the wells for an endless supply of water. Of course in the wet we have more than enough water. There are courses that fill up and even overflow and flood the plains. But usually the water stays in the channels. Then the land blooms in flowers so pretty, you want to stay out all day and to enjoy them."

Rennie looked around, trying to envision the wet season. She couldn't wait to see how it all looked.

Smiling, she studied some of the cattle.

"Those are the shorthorns you were telling me about."

Hunter nodded. "Yes, they give a good ratio of beef to the total poundage."

"Let's not get too near them," Daphne said nervously, coming up beside Hunter. "They won't stampede, will they?"

"Not unless something spooks them, and it's highly unlikely on a hot day like today. They're too lethargic."

Yet Rennie knew they could. It was unlikely, but she remembered Hunter's recent accident.

"Do you rotate the fields for graze or does the herd move naturally?" Rennie asked. She knew that depletion of the grazing land was a real concern and wondered how Hunter handled it. There was so much to learn about ranching in Australia.

"We watch to see how the grass holds up. If it's getting used up and the cattle aren't moving naturally then we force it. Usually, however, they keep roaming. We have enough bores that the entire station is adequately covered, so water isn't a concern."

"When do you have roundup?" she asked.

Looking up, she met the anger in Daphne's eyes. Startled, she stared at the younger woman for a long moment. Then realization struck and Rennie looked away before a huge smile broke out.

Daphne resented her knowledge about cattle. Heavens, it was little enough, yet more than Daphne knew.

"Roundups in the spring and fall. We brand the calves in the spring, cull the herd in the fall. Sometimes we sell early if the year's bad and the land's getting depleted," Hunter said.

"It's hard to believe that the steaks we have in Sydney come from cows like that," Daphne said, uncomfortably walking on the uneven ground.

She kept a wary eye on the cattle.

"Steers," Hunter corrected her.

"And not only steak; there are a lot of other by-products from cattle, using the horns and hoof, the hide," Rennie said, eyeing the other woman.

She couldn't help the small spurt of delight she felt with the new knowledge that she was more suited to be a wife to Hunter than someone like Daphne.

Hunter glanced between the two women, his lips twitching slightly.

"Showing off?" he said softly to Rennie, raising one eyebrow.

She caught her breath at his look and nodded, a small smile touching her lips.

"At least you're not merely another pretty face," he said blandly, brushing the back of his fingers across her cheek, then he turned back toward the truck.

Rennie cherished the warm glow, and tried to hold on to the feeling as Daphne continued to stumble and rub up against Hunter, and her husband remained silently acquiescent.

Stuart had never called her pretty. Hunter had several times. Maybe she could ignore Daphne, especially if he called her pretty again.

Her own decision to ignore the other woman had been impossible to keep. By the time they reached the homestead in the late afternoon, she was fed up with Daphne's flirting and her husband's tolerance.

True, he did nothing to encourage her, but neither did he rebuff her in any fashion. Rennie seethed silently, wishing she could demand that she be allowed to sit by Hunter. Wishing he'd insist. Wishing he'd tell Daphne that he was married and to keep her hands to herself.

If anything, Hunter appeared amused by both women. His gaze had touched on Rennie several times when they'd stopped to view different parts of the station, and she knew he was amused. Yet he seemed just as amused at Daphne's attempts to draw closer. Blast but the man made her mad.

George met them when they drove in, leaning negligently against the support post on the back porch, watching Rennie as she climbed down from the Ute and stormed toward the house. When Hunter and Daphne were close enough to hear, George spoke to her.

"You got a present delivered today, Rennie," he said, his eyes flicking to Hunter, then back to her.

"A present? From whom?" It wasn't her birthday. Why would anyone send her a present? Had Gram sent something?

"Set them out front, near the porch."

"What is it?" Hunter asked, his face drawn in harsh lines again.

George shrugged, his eyes never leaving Rennie's.

"I left them around front."

Curious, she hurried around the house, and paused as she saw the rose bushes that leaned against the veranda. There were four, already in bloom, with large blossoms, two reds, a white and a pink.

"Oh, how lovely!" She leaned over to inhale their fragrance, her fingers lightly touching the delicate petals.

"My, my, your friend from town, undoubtedly," Daphne drawled when she saw the roses.

Hunter frowned at her. "What do you mean?"

"Rennie made a big fuss about how much she liked roses when Gerry Dalton was here. Obviously he's trying to please the lady," she said smugly.

"Are they from Gerry?" Hunter asked his grandfather, standing still and poised.

George shrugged.

Rennie saw the card tucked into one bush and reached for it, her trepidation building. She hoped they weren't from Gerry. That'd cause more trouble.

Yet she couldn't imagine who else would think to send her rose bushes. He'd been the only one she'd discussed her plans for a garden with.

To give you a start on your garden. These will only enhance the beauty of the outback in your eyes. Gerry.

She swallowed and turned to face Hunter. His anger was almost tangible. Slowly she held out the note. He snapped it from her fingers and read it, crushing the paper into a ball when he'd finished.

Rennie knew he was angry, but she'd done nothing wrong, and she wasn't going to be made to feel guilty.

"I thought you were going to take care of him," she said.

Hunter's narrowed eyes met hers and he stared at her for a long moment.

"I thought I'd wait until I went into town, but I see I underestimated the attraction."

"Hunter, they're roses. I mentioned I liked roses and wanted to start a garden once I had the house redecorated," she explained. "He's being neighborly by sending them."

"You're my wife, Rennie. If you want rose bushes, I'll buy them for you. Throw these away."

"Throw them away! They're beautiful. I can't throw them away."

"Maybe they have a special meaning after all," Daphne murmured stepping closer to Hunter.

"Shut up, Daphne. This discussion is between my

husband and me. I sure don't need your snippy comments making the situation worse!" Rennie almost shouted in her frustration.

It was an awkward enough situation without Daphne intruding.

"Rennie, that was inexcusably rude. Daphne is our guest. Apologize at once," Hunter ordered.

She took a deep breath, her eyes never leaving his, defiance sparkling in her eyes. Briefly she wondered what he would do if she defied him. But he was right—she had been rude.

"Excuse me, Daphne. I should not have spoken to you that way."

Rennie turned and ran up the shallow steps to the veranda and into the house. The door slammed behind her and she didn't even notice.

She was already running up the stairs, tears hampering her vision. Hearing the strong stride behind her, she ran faster, gaining their bedroom just as Hunter's hand reached out and jerked her to a halt. He hesitated a moment, then almost dragged her into the bedroom, shutting the door behind him.

"I told Grandpa to get rid of them," he said, his teeth gritted in anger.

"It's not the roses" fault. They're so pretty. I don't want them thrown away," she said, trying to ease her arm from his tight grip, wanting to ease away from the anger radiating from him.

She blinked at the tears, his face blurred before her.

"I won't have Gerry Dalton's flowers greeting me every time I come home. Dammit, Tessa tried these games with

Alex and made his life hell. I won't tolerate anything like that from you, is that clear?"

His thumb came up to brush one fallen tear from her cheek, his expression implacable.

"I'm not playing any games. I didn't ask him to send me flowers. I never even asked to meet him. You said you'd take care of things. Do it and stop blaming me!"

She was almost shouting again.

It was all unfair. She had no interest in Gerry Dalton. Why was he constantly causing problems between her and Hunter?

"The second thing I won't tolerate is your rudeness to Daphne. Hell, she is our guest—my guest, if you don't want to be involved. I'm trying to make sure the Adams don't have a case to contest the custody issue. Your being rude and difficult isn't helping to demonstrate the kind of atmosphere suitable for raising a child."

"Take her side of it. You've known her longer. Maybe you should have thought about taking up with her again and marrying her after Tessa and Alex died. That's obviously what she wants."

She pulled again, but his hand was firmly wrapped around her arm, and she couldn't budge an inch.

He leaned over until his nose almost touched hers, his fiery slate eyes almost melting her with smoldering heat.

"I'm married to you. For all time. Daphne is leaving soon, but you will remain here and you will stay the hell away from Gerry Dalton!"

He flung her arm away as if it were distasteful and turned, quickly leaving the room.

Rennie remained where she was, absently rubbing her

arm, stunned at the force of his anger. She listened to his footsteps as he descended the stairs. The banging of the door let her know that he'd gone outside. A moment later she heard the murmur of voices from the veranda, but refused to eavesdrop. He'd made himself perfectly clear. She didn't need to hear any more.

Dinner was strained. Rennie served the stew that had been simmering all day, adding fresh rolls and a crisp salad. She ate without speaking and did her best to ignore the conversation that rose around her. A quick glance at the veranda prior to dinner had shown her that the roses were gone. What had George done with them?

Daphne enthused about her sightseeing expedition that day, and told amusing stories of incidents in Sydney. Hunter remained silent at Rennie's side, but George laughed at her anecdotes and eased into telling tales about the early days on Silver Creek Station.

"Want to help me give Kerry her bath, Hunter? She's about as dirty as we were when we returned this afternoon," Daphne said gaily as the last of the apple pie was consumed.

She'd ignored Rennie throughout the meal.

He flicked a glance at Rennie, but her gaze remained on her plate.

"Sure. We can read her a story after the bath. She likes that book you brought."

Rennie bit her lip in an effort to refrain from saying anything.

Prior to her arrival, Kerry had no toys or books.

But he had never made mention of the dolly and blocks she'd bought. Only the gifts from Daphne.

After the dishes were put up, Rennie walked out to the veranda. It was empty. George was in the office, Hunter and Daphne upstairs with Kerry. She sank down on the rocker for a while, moving to and fro slowly, trying to regain some sense of peace.

How had everything gone so wrong in such a short time? And without her doing anything.

Finally, she rose and headed for the barn. She searched the area around the outbuildings until she found the bushes tossed in a heap on a pile of manure. Gently she eased them away, stood them beside the weathered barn wall. Several branches had been broken, and dust and dried manure dusted the leaves. But otherwise the plants were still sturdy. Tomorrow she'd return them.

Heading back to the house, her mind made up, she hesitated when she heard George's voice on the veranda. When Daphne answered, Rennie turned and entered the house through the kitchen. Silently she made her way to bed.

She feigned sleep when Hunter came to bed some hours later. She wasn't up to any more confrontations. She almost exclaimed aloud when he slid beneath the sheet and reached over to draw her up against him. Settling her beside him, his arm across her stomach, he was asleep in only moments.

Rennie lay in stunned silence. Did he always hold her as she slept? Gradually the warmth of his body soothed hers, and the sheer strength of him made her feel sheltered and cherished. She drifted to sleep.

* * *

It would be impossible to keep her trip to town a secret from Daphne, so Rennie didn't even try. Immediately after breakfast, she brought the car around to the barn and loaded the plants into the back. Stopping by the house, she picked up Kerry. Meeting Daphne's surprised look, Rennie calmly told her she had errands to run and left.

She returned to the homestead late in the afternoon. She'd deliberately stayed as long as possible in Boolong Creek visiting with Mamie Jordan at her nursery, not wishing to spend any time alone with Daphne.

She hoped she was back before Hunter. It was important that she be the one to tell Hunter what she'd done.

Daphne would embellish the situation intolerably.

The homestead appeared deserted when Rennie drew up. She carried Kerry into the kitchen to began preparing supper. The baby played on the floor, banging pot lids and pretending to stir things with a wooden spoon.

Rennie kept a wary eye out for Hunter. She didn't want to guess at his reaction when he found out what she'd done. She only hoped they could have some privacy. It was in short supply around this place.

Time crept slowly by and Rennie grew more and more nervous. Where was he? She wished he'd hurry up. As the dinner hour drew near, they had less and less time to discuss anything with any privacy.

Yet when he rode up she almost panicked. She watched from the kitchen window as Hunter dismounted and led the horse into the big barn. It seemed as if only seconds passed before he was striding toward the house, dusty, tired, and sexy enough to make her mouth water.

Rennie watched as he approached and, rubbing her hands against her jeans, she turned to face him when he entered the kitchen.

"Hunter." Was that voice hers?

He smiled at her, nodded, and hunkered down to see to Kerry.

Rennie cleared her throat and moved slowly toward him.

"Hunter, I took the roses back," she said all in a rush.

He looked up, puzzled.

"What?"

Slowly he rose. Taking a step closer, he almost touched her.

"What do you mean you took them back?"

She met his gaze.

"They were beautiful plants that didn't need to be destroyed just because you didn't like who sent them. I returned them to Mamie Jordan."

"I thought Grandpa threw them away."

"I rescued them."

"Rescued them. Bloody hell! Did they mean that much to you?"

"No. They didn't mean anything to me. But they were pretty plants that had meant something to whoever grew them. Mamie was pleased to see them, since I couldn't use them. I'm not sorry I took them back."

"I told you..."

"You never told me not to return them to the grower. Hunter, they were so pretty, I didn't want them just to die in a manure heap."

He stared down at her in disbelief, slowly shaking his head.

"You are one headstrong woman. What am I going to do with you?"

She took a breath and started to reply but his mouth cut her off as he claimed hers in a sultry kiss.

His lips molded themselves to her, hot and pressing. He moved them against hers, drawing out an involuntary response. Slowly his tongue traced the seam of her mouth, slipped inside to taste the sweetness there.

Rennie slowly let out her breath as his mouth wreaked havoc of another sort. He only touched her mouth, yet the flames of passion were already rising throughout her body. She longed to step closer, to feel the latent strength of him, to have him inflame her entirely.

But she couldn't move; she could only hold on to the reality of his kiss, knew that without it she would be nothing.

"Oh, sorry, didn't mean to intrude," Daphne said, coming to a stop inside the door, her eyes avidly taking in the scene.

Slowly Hunter raised his head, his eyes boring deeply into Rennie's, ignoring Daphne completely. Without another word, he turned and left the room, heading for the shower.

"No intrusion," Rennie said breezily, hoping Daphne couldn't see her frantic heart rate.

She turned back to the counter to resume cooking.

"I was just greeting my husband after a day apart."

"How touching," Daphne said, pulling out a kitchen chair and sitting down.

Rennie didn't want her to stay, but didn't know how to get rid of her without being rude. And she knew what that'd get her.

"I wonder if he'll feel so amorous when he learns you

went into town to see Gerry today?" Daphne said maliciously. "Won't he find that interesting?"

Rennie turned to face her, for once feeling in control.

"I've already explained to Hunter that I returned the rose bushes. And I spent the day at Mamie Jordan's exploring her garden and getting advice for growing things here on the outback. You're free to check with her if you doubt me. Hunter can too, for all I care. I did not see Gerry Dalton."

Daphne said nothing for a moment, dropping her gaze to Kerry and watching the little girl play with the pans.

Then, "Doesn't she have any real toys?" she asked.

"Of course, but she likes to bang on the pans when I'm cooking."

Rennie wished that someone would come and entertain Daphne. Even grumpy George would be welcomed now.

"We'll have lots of toys for her when she comes to stay with us. She won't have to make do with old pans," Daphne said smoothly.

Rennie glared at her, puzzled.

"What do you mean?"

"When Kerry comes to Sydney. Didn't Hunter tell you? He doesn't want to keep that side of her family away from her."

"I didn't know you were planning to take her for a visit. When?"

"I haven't decided yet. It really doesn't concern you, does it? I'm her aunt."

"I'm also her aunt, by marriage. And when the adoption goes through I'll be her mother."

Rennie held on to her temper, but it was hard.

"Early days to be talking about adoption," Daphne drawled.

She rose gracefully and smiled at Rennie.

"Can I help with dinner?"

"I have everything under control," Rennie said, still staring at her.

What did she mean, early days? Hadn't Hunter already started the proceedings?

Was Daphne hinting that there'd be some problems with the adoption?

"You may think so, but I doubt it."

With a casual wave, Daphne sauntered from the room.

Rennie took a deep breath and tried to relax. That woman drove her crazy. Surely Hunter would tell her if Kerry was going away.

It was at dinner that Daphne dropped her bombshell.

"You know, Hunter, I think I'll stay a little longer after all and go on that camping trip with you," she said guilelessly.

His head came up and he stared at her silently for a moment. Then, nodding, he said easily, "Fine. We can leave the day after tomorrow. We'll be gone a few nights. You up to that much horseback riding?"

Rennie felt sick. What camping trip? Hunter had invited Daphne on a camping trip? How could he?

9

"Sure, I'll be the best drover you've got," Daphne replied saucily.

"Moving it up, aren't you? Expecting me and Rennie, too?" George asked, pausing in his eating while he studied his grandson.

"Of course."

"What camping trip?" Rennie asked, still at a loss.

"Riding south to check out a portion of the herd grazing down there. It'll take several days because of the distance. If we were going further, I'd fly down to one of the other houses. This way you can see more of the station and get a chance to camp out."

"Someone needs to watch Kerry," Daphne said, frowning as if the thought of Rennie's departure didn't meet her plan.

"No problem," George said. "Maggie helped care for Kerry before Rennie came. I reckon she can watch her for a few days."

Rennie was annoyed that Hunter had discussed the drive with Daphne and never even mentioned it to her. Her gaze dropped to her plate. How could he have discussed it to Daphne first? Theirs might be a marriage of convenience, but the convenience wasn't all going to be on his side.

"Hunter, will you help me clear the table?" Rennie asked

when everyone had finished eating, not caring if the edge in her voice gave away her frustrated feelings.

She was tired of being left out or ignored. She was going to have it out with him tonight. Her emotions were too raw for them to continue as they had been.

He looked surprised at her request.

"Dishes are women's work," George grumbled.

"Don't be silly, who did them before I came?"

Rennie turned on him, anger flaring.

No wonder Tessa hadn't been happy here. Had she and Alex ever been left alone?

"We did, of course. Grandpa, I can manage my own life. I'll clear, Rennie can wash. You and Daphne take Kerry on the veranda."

Hunter rose and reached for a plate. Making effective work of stacking the dishes, he led the way into the kitchen.

Rennie started water in the sink and reached to take the dishes from him.

"You don't want help with the dishes, Rennie. What do you want?" he said, standing close, crowding her with his proximity.

Rennie felt the heat from his body surround her. His tanned face was somber as he watched her, his eyes silvery. She took a breath; he smelled of soap and tangy spice and his unique male scent. Dumping the dishes in the water, she tried to frame her thoughts so that she wouldn't upset him.

But she wanted some answers, no matter what the result.

"Did you invite Daphne on a camping trip?"

He reached out and clasped his hands on her shoulders, turning her to face him, drawing her up close. Rennie tilted her head to see him better, her eyes accusing.

"I mentioned to her the first night she was here that sometimes we go out several days at a time when checking the area south of us. I said if she was here some time when we went she could go along." He shook his head. "I did not, however, invite her on this next drive. I wasn't even planning to go for another couple of weeks. You heard George ask if we were moving it up. It'll take a day to get provisions and things. We can leave the day after tomorrow, be gone three days or so and then she'll be on her way back to Sydney."

"Why bother? Wouldn't she leave sooner if there were no drive?"

She wished she could have kept the petulance from her tone.

"I'm trying to clear up some things," he said vaguely.

His thumbs traced the delicate skin over her collarbone, sending shivering waves of tingling awareness through her. Her body craved more.

She wished he'd lean down and kiss her, wished he'd take her up to their room and make love to her. For a while she'd be able to pretend that he cared for her and wanted her. That they didn't have a business arrangement.

That Daphne wasn't wreaking havoc on her peace of mind.

"About Kerry?" she asked breathlessly.

"Yes. Among other things. But Daphne won't be here long. You'll enjoy the ride. You said you used to ride all the time in Texas. Have you camped out before?"

"Yes. Do you really want me to go?"

She wished he'd invited her before Daphne, not made it

sound like an afterthought to include her and George.

"I need you to go. You wouldn't leave me out there alone with that she-cat on the prowl, now would you?"

Amusement danced in his eyes.

"On the prowl?"

She licked her lips, took a deep breath. Why was it so hard to concentrate? Although the touch of his hands was driving her wild, surely she could rise above that and focus on what he was saying.

"Don't worry about it. I can handle Daphne. I want you to come. Can you ride that long, days at a time?"

"Of course. You can't be from Texas and not ride," she said sassily, her hands coming up and resting hesitantly against his chest, absorbing the heat from beneath his cotton shirt, her own pulse matching the steady pounding of his heart.

Suddenly the intimacy between them, the strong attraction she had for her husband washed through her—the warm kitchen, the quiet humming of the refrigerator.

Sighing softly, Rennie leaned forward slightly, her head tilted back for a kiss. Hunter pulled her into his arms, trapping her hands against his chest. He lowered his face to hers, his breath mingling with hers as his silvery eyes stared deeply into her smoky blue ones. She felt the shimmering desire flood her and smiled slightly as he closed the slight distance between them and covered her lips with his.

He deepened the kiss immediately, opening her mouth. His lips were hot and urgent and his tongue made deep strokes as he plunged into her sweet heat. She met his touch, mated her tongue with his, her body growing hotter and hotter.

Slowly her hands crept up to his shoulders, encircling him,

pulling herself tightly against him, relishing the sensation of the strong muscles of his chest igniting the fire that burned deep within her. Her fingers trailed across the strength of his shoulders, kneading the corded muscles, finding the thickness of his hair, tangling with the dark strands. She loved him so much.

He adjusted his body against hers, his hands pressing her hips into his. Shocked a bit by the obvious state of his desire, she reveled in the knowledge that she could cause such a reaction. She didn't trust the durability of the attraction, but for today it was enough. The future must take care of itself.

He eased the kiss to an end and rested his forehead on hers as his eyes flicked to her slightly swollen lips.

"Finish the dishes and we can continue this upstairs."

Rennie was pleased to note that she wasn't the only one affected by their kiss. Nodding shyly, she began to release her hold on him. But his hands didn't move. He continued to hold her against him, as if he also relished the feel of their bodies touching, the heat and desire that raged between them.

"I can't do the dishes like this," she said softly, knowing that the happiness that filled her must show.

With an exaggerated sigh, he dropped a quick kiss on her lips and released her.

"I'll clear the rest of the table," he said, turning away.

The task had never been done so fast. But Rennie knew they couldn't slip upstairs when they were finished. There were too many people around and they had obligations toward their guest. But it was fun to dream about it.

Maybe Tessa would have been happier had she'd a house of her own.

If she and Hunter had their own place, they could do anything they wanted, anywhere they wanted.

A vision of Hunter making love to her in the kitchen flooded her mind and she could feel the heat rise in her face.

"Now what?" Hunter asked laconically.

He sat on one of the kitchen chairs, his legs sprawled out in front of him, hands laced on his flat belly, watching her work. He'd seen the color stain her cheeks.

"Nothing."

Good grief, she couldn't tell him what she was thinking. She had no business thinking such thoughts anyway.

"Rennie."

His voice was low but intense. She looked over.

"We're married–you can tell me anything."

Her eyes met his for a long moment, then she turned back to the sink.

"Not yet, I can't," she murmured.

She felt him rise and cross the room, though he was quite silent for so large a man. His hands on her shoulders startled her.

"What does that mean?"

He leaned his face down next to hers, his cheek almost touching hers.

She kept her gaze firmly on the dishes.

"I'm not used to sharing a lot of my thoughts, you know. Except for the few years I lived with my grandmother, no one was especially interested in anything I thought. And she was grateful I was there. You and I don't know each other very well yet."

"But we can learn about each other. Share our thoughts," he murmured in her.

Turning her head slightly, she leaned back against him, her hands dripping water.

"And you'll share your thoughts with me?"

He kissed her gently.

"I'll try."

His slow smile lit his face.

"I guess I'm not used to it any more than you are. But I can learn, just as you can. What caused you to blush?"

She blushed again, wanting to look away, but, mesmerized by the gentle look he gave her, she was unable to. Swallowing hard, she shook her head.

"It's silly."

"Tell me."

Exasperated, she turned back to the sink.

"Okay I was thinking if we lived alone we wouldn't have to hurry with the dishes so we could go upstairs. You could make love to me right in the kitchen."

He laughed and hugged her tightly.

"No wonder Alex kept talking about getting a place for him and Tessa. I never truly understood why until now. Forget the damned dishes."

He released her and took her wet hand, pulling her across the room.

"Hunter, stop—what are you doing?"

Rennie had to run to keep up with his long stride.

"Taking my wife to bed," he said.

"Not now."

She tried to hold back, but his grip was strong.

"Why not now?" he asked.

They reached the stairs and he hurried her up them and

into their room. Shutting the door behind them, he drew her into his arms, pressing himself against her as his mouth came down to claim hers in a hot, erotic kiss.

* * *

Two days later Rennie was awakened early by Hunter.

"Time to get up. I want to leave early so we can get some traveling done while it's still cool."

Hunter brushed her hair away from her face. He was already dressed, the light from the bathroom spilling into the bedroom. It was still dark outside.

She blinked the sleep from her eyes and nodded. "I'll be down in a few minutes."

"Wear a long-sleeved shirt; you're too fair to be out in the sun all day and not get severely burned."

"Won't that be hot?" she asked.

"Not as bad as sunburn. It'll shade your skin. I've got a hat for you."

He bent his head to kiss her lightly on the lips, then rose and left, his boots sounding loud in the early morning stillness. Were the others awake yet? she wondered.

She was the last to arrive in the kitchen. George and Daphne were finishing eggs and bacon, Hunter was leaning against the counter sipping coffee. Maggie Taylor was cooking at the big stove. She gave Rennie a cheerful smile in greeting.

"Sorry if I'm late."

Rennie looked at the almost empty breakfast plates.

"You're not. You've time to eat," Hunter said as Maggie dished her up some eggs and popped some bread into the toaster. "Jacko's saddling up the horses and Phil has already loaded the pack animals. We'll start as soon as everyone's ready."

Daphne looked tired and dazed at being up so early, but stunning in her designer jeans. George calmly ate his meal, ignoring everyone. Were any of them morning people beside Hunter Rennie wondered as she sat down to eat.

She wasn't very hungry so early, but it would be a long time before they stopped for lunch.

They left the homestead as dawn was breaking. The sky was beautifully clear. Slowly the edge of the eastern horizon changed from black to mauve, to pink then to the shining brightness of early sun. The air was crisp and fresh.

Hunter led the way. Daphne quickly maneuvered her horse next to his and began asking questions about the plants she saw.

Rennie felt the familiar rise of jealousy at the sight, and wished Hunter had sought her out and pointed out the plants to her. She was the newcomer to Australia. But she couldn't bring herself to join them.

George fell in beside Rennie. The other drovers paired up behind them, keeping their horses at a walk.

"Hunter tells me you took the roses back to Mamie Jordan's," George said as they rode along.

Rennie was watching Hunter talk to Daphne and didn't reply at first. She glanced over and nodded.

"That's right."

Was she going to get more grief over the episode?

"What did you tell Gerry?" he asked.

"I haven't told him anything. I suppose I should write him

a note and thank him for the thought," she said pensively. "It's rude just to ignore the gesture."

"He drove a wedge between Tessa and Alex, you know," George said.

"So Hunter said. But maybe it wasn't all one-sided. I'm beginning to understand a little of how Tessa must have felt."

"Knew you wouldn't stay the course," he said with satisfaction.

She swirled around at him, her eyes blazing.

"Now you listen to me, George Bradshaw, you don't know anything of the sort. I *will* stay the course. I'm married to Hunter and I plan to stay that way. But it's hard to be newly married, especially with the kind of marriage we have and not have any privacy. Did you ever think about that? You know if I'm taking a shower or in with Kerry, or..."

She trailed off, embarrassed at where her words were taking her.

"Of if you and Hunter are making love," George chuckled.

"Yes. It makes things damn awkward," she blurted out.

He watched the couple ahead of them, lost in thought for a long moment. Then he nodded.

"I can see that it might. Especially with someone like you. You're not used to men and don't have a high opinion of them to start with."

"No more so than you and Hunter seem to have about women," she returned.

"True, but we've got cause."

"And I don't?"

"Hunter doesn't know much about a woman's love.

Doesn't realize how powerful it can be and how much a man craves it once he's experienced it."

She didn't respond.

"You're in love with him and it shows. One day he'll see it," George said. "Daphne's seen it. She doesn't like it either."

"He doesn't want me to be in love with him," she said stiffly.

Was she such an open book?

"Only because he doesn't know about love. His mother left when he was a little boy. His own fiancée betrayed him with another man. Tessa wasn't strong enough for Alex. Those are the only examples of a woman's *love* he's seen."

She looked sharply at the older man.

"Are you selling Hunter to me?"

George met her gaze.

"Maybe just explaining him to you."

She searched his eyes for a hidden meaning, but couldn't find anything but honest regard. She nodded and turned back to watch where they were going, her thoughts tumbling.

It was true, Hunter hadn't had good experiences with women and love. But neither had she.

Yet she knew she loved him. This feeling was so much stronger than what she'd felt for Stuart. So different, so right.

Could he learn to love her given time? Or at least have some affection for her?

Tears filled her eyes as she watched him riding in front of her, jealousy of Daphne threatening to swamp her.

Why couldn't he want to ride with his wife? She wanted him to so much.

He rode with indolent grace, moving with the horse, a part

of the beast. He looked as comfortable and at ease on horseback as he did in his bedroom. She loved watching him, would never tire of it. His broad shoulders were strong enough for a woman to depend upon all her life. He was all male, strong, competent, successful.

Yet capable of gentleness. One only had to witness how he related to his niece. A man of strong commitments. It wasn't easy taking on someone else's child. He'd made sacrifices for that child. He was quiet but missed nothing.

How could he miss how she felt for him?

Maybe he hadn't missed it. Maybe he suspected that she loved him, but didn't want to embarrass her by mentioning it since he couldn't return that love.

Kicking her horse, she moved up on Hunter's right side.

"Having fun?" he asked as she drew level.

"Yes. Though I expect I'll be sore tonight. It's been a while since I've ridden all day."

"We'll all be tired tonight," Daphne said, looking archly at Hunter. "I hope you brought some liniment, Hunter," she purred.

Rennie knew that Daphne would expect Hunter to help her with the liniment.

Over her dead body!

"How far will we ride today?" Rennie asked.

"Eight or ten hours. Want to check out some of the bores south of here, see how many cattle have drifted from one pasture to another."

"And the next day?"

"We'll keep on south until we cover the bores I want to double-check. Tally the cattle in the area. We'll make a wide sweep, then return home. Up to riding a little faster?"

Rennie grinned and nodded. She loved riding. As part of her job with the cattleman's association she'd had access to horses and had ridden whenever she could, taking advantage of the perk.

She had missed riding since coming to Australia.

"Daphne, you'd better pair up with Grandpa. We're going on ahead," Hunter said, touching the side of his mount.

Rennie smiled in delight and urged her horse onward. Soon they were flying across the ground, the thundering hoofs the only sound in the silent morning.

Daphne, George and the drovers were quickly left behind as they rode side by side across the outback.

Reining in their blowing horses some time later, Rennie laughed in sheer delight.

"That was great!"

"You're a good rider. I'll get you your own horse," Hunter said as they settled down to walk.

"Not much time to ride, with Kerry," she said, patting the damp neck of her mount.

"Someone's usually around when she's napping. It's the hot part of the day, but you might get some riding in. Or we can ride evenings if you like."

She nodded but didn't make any commitment. She knew he was tired at the end of the day. The last thing he'd want was to be on a horse again.

Still, she was touched by the offer.

When they came upon a copse of scrawny acacia, Hunter pulled up and dismounted in the scant shade.

"We'll wait here for the others. After lunch we'll go on. I

plan to stop near a particular bore tonight for camp. I want to make sure we reach it before dark."

They sat in the meager shade and talked while they waited for the others to catch up.

Hunter told her more about the station, the problems they faced, the ways he or his grandfather had dealt with situations in the past. He questioned her about her work in Texas, learned more of what she knew about cattle.

Rennie was sorry when the rest of the group arrived.

They reached the bore Hunter had mentioned in the late afternoon. The men quickly set up camp, then left to scout the cattle in the area. Rennie started dinner while Daphne sat near by, complaining of aching muscles.

Once the men returned, however, her manner changed dramatically. Instantly she was cheerful and enthusiastic about the trip, intrigued by the camp. She sat next to Hunter, telling him how much she was enjoying herself.

Rennie was tired. The day had been long and she wasn't used to cooking over an open fire. The meal had turned out fine, for which she was grateful. The praise for dinner was welcomed, both for the warm feeling she got at the praise and the flash of jealousy in Daphne's eyes.

"Do you make these camping trips often, Hunter?" Daphne asked as she sat back with a cup of coffee.

George and Hunter had brought the sleeping-bags near the fire, but no one was tired enough to sleep yet.

"Several times a year," he said, settling down with a cup of his own, his eyes on his wife.

"With so many drovers?"

"Depends on what we're doing. This time I want to cover

as much ground as possible in a little amount of time. Other times it might just be a couple of us."

"And do you always stay out for several days?"

Daphne persisted, trying to claim his attention.

Rennie glanced up, met the silvery heat in Hunter's gaze, feeling for a moment as if the rest of the camp had vanished into a mist and there was only her and Hunter.

"Usually. It's a big station. When we want to see the southernmost part, we get Ben to fly us down to the southern homestead. I have a foreman and his family there who maintain that part of the station," he replied carelessly, his gaze still locked with Rennie's.

"Is the house down there as big as the one you have?"

"No. The main homestead is the big house."

"Needs fixing up. I could help with that, if you like," she offered.

"Rennie will see to it," Hunter said easily, a slight smile softening his features.

Rennie felt the wash of heat sweep through her and she smiled shyly in return.

"It's Rennie's home, only right she be the one to fix it up the way she wants," George said suddenly from across the fire.

All eyes swiveled to him.

Rennie was stunned. George was defending her? He called it her home? George? She couldn't believe it.

"That's right," Hunter confirmed, his eyes unreadable across the flickering flames.

Rennie was touched that George had stood up for her. Maybe there was hope from that quarter after all.

"I'm getting tired. Did you bring that liniment?" Daphne asked. "I'm not used to riding so far in a day."

Hunter nodded.

"I'll get it for you."

He rose easily and went to the camp supplies. Returning, he tossed her a bottle.

"Hope it works. Come on, Rennie, time for bed."

She looked up unexpectedly. "What?"

Hunter snagged two sleeping-bags and tucked them beneath his arm. With his other hand he reached out for her.

"Bed. You look as if you're about to fall asleep where you sit."

She took his hand and rose, looking around.

"Where?"

He walked away from the fire, his hand tight around hers.

"Where are we going?" She glanced over her shoulder to see everyone watching them. "Hunter, for heaven's sake, where are we going?"

"We're finding a place away from everyone else. Don't worry, they all know we're still on our honeymoon."

"Oh, Hunter," she groaned in embarrassment. "Now everyone will think..."

She couldn't finish her sentence.

"Hunter, stop," she hissed, tugging on his hand.

"When we're far enough away. And that's exactly what I want everyone to think."

He walked steadily out across the desolate land, his stride long, firm, sure. Soon the camp fire was a flickering dot behind them. No sounds from the camp carried this far; there was only the soft whisper of the evening wind against the spiny grass.

"This is far enough," Hunter finally said with satisfaction, dumping the two sleeping-bags.

"There wasn't any need to come this far," Rennie said petulantly. "We're only going to sleep, for heaven's sake."

"No, sweetheart, we're not only going to sleep."

In the distance a howl rose, then another. Rennie shivered slightly and stepped closer. "What's that?"

"Dingoes. They're not close, and won't bother us tonight. Nothing will bother us tonight."

He reached out to draw her into his arms.

"Hunter, why are you doing this?" Rennie asked, already wanting him more than she ever had before.

"Is it just to show Daphne?"

She couldn't bear it if that was the only reason.

His mouth came down to cover hers.

The next morning the group spread out as they rode south checking on the cattle. Hunter paired up the group, assigning Rennie to ride with George.

She complied without question, but when they were mounted she realized that Hunter was going with Daphne. Her heart sank and she turned away without a word.

She and George rode west first, then south. He pointed out groups of cattle, and explained a bit about how they mustered them for roundups. Talk centered on the station and cattle which Rennie found interesting.

She only wished Hunter had been riding with her instead of George. Why had he chosen Daphne?

"You holding up all right?" George asked when they rested for lunch.

Rennie smiled and nodded.

"Though I have muscles aching that I didn't even know I had."

"You'll need to keep in shape if you want to travel with Hunter on these drives. He makes several a year. Anna used to go with me."

He gazed off across the bush, lost in thought.

"That was so long ago."

"Tell me about her," she said gently, wondering if Hunter would want her to come with him on future drives.

Why had he chosen Daphne to ride with him? To keep her sweet so that she wouldn't cause problems with Kerry? Or for other reasons?

She shivered slightly despite the sun's warmth, and listened as George began to reminisce.

Late that afternoon they reached the designated campsite. Jacko and Phil were already setting up camp. The others hadn't come in yet.

Rennie sank tiredly near the small fire and watched dully as Jacko cooked the evening meal, glad that Hunter had rotated the task. She was almost too tired to eat. Longing for sleep, she wondered if she had time for a nap before dinner.

The other drovers arrived in ones and twos and took care of their horses, penning them in a makeshift corral for the night.

Jacko served the dinner.

Wondering where Hunter and Daphne were, Rennie began to eat.

As they were finishing, Hunter and Daphne rode into camp.

Rennie's eyes moved between them, noting the smug, satisfied look on Daphne's face, the closed, tight expression on Hunter's.

"Enjoy your day?" Hunter asked as he sat beside her, his plate heaped with hot stew.

She nodded, shifting away from him slightly. She looked over to Daphne, frowning when she saw the possessive looks that the other woman was casting at Hunter.

"You were gone a long time," Rennie said casually, her eyes refusing to meet Hunter's.

"Daphne can't ride fast."

His tone gave nothing away.

Rennie wondered if he was unhappy with his guest or just resigned to the fact that a city dweller couldn't ride like those on the station.

"You and Grandpa get on okay?" he asked.

Rennie nodded.

They'd done fine, she realized. No grumbles from George, no complaining, and no new attacks on her. And she'd caught a glimpse of the man's loneliness when he'd spoken of his long-dead wife.

She sipped her coffee but the caffeine didn't make her any more alert. She was so tired and her body ached from riding steadily for two days. She longed for her sleeping-bag and the oblivion of sleep.

"We had a wonderful day, didn't we Hunter?"

Daphne sat down beside him and smiled smugly at Rennie.

"I learned so much. I can't wait for tomorrow. Hunter said he'd show me where there's a natural pond that's not artesian, so the water won't be minerally."

Hunter nodded then rose to get some coffee.

"Maybe we'll go swimming," Daphne confided to Rennie,

dropping her voice slightly. "It gets so hot during the middle of the day."

"I didn't know you brought a suit," Rennie said, wishing wistfully that Hunter had invited her to go swimming. It did get hot at midday.

Daphne giggled softly, her eyes tracking Hunter.

"I didn't. It won't be the first time I've gone skinny-dipping, nor Hunter's first time, I bet."

Rennie stiffened. How dared Hunter not offer the same chance to her? And he'd better not be going skinny-dipping with anyone. He was married to her and he'd better remember that.

Incensed, Rennie rose lithely and stormed over to Hunter, who had stopped to talk to Jacko.

"I want a word with you," she said icily.

"In a minute. Let me finish with Jacko," he replied, studying her expression for a moment before turning back to the other man.

She nodded and dumped her dish into the pan of soapy water. As she stood beside the men while they talked and ate, her sense of outrage grew. How dared he spend the day with Daphne? He should be making it clear to her that he was married and putting up a united front with his wife.

10

"All right, let's hear it."

Hunter tossed his plate into the dishwater and took her hand, walking her away from the camp fire.

"You look mad enough to spit nails, Rennie."

His voice was slightly amused.

She glared at him.

"You would be too if you found me out fooling around with someone else, wouldn't you?"

He stopped and spun her around until she faced him, leaning over to look deep into her eyes.

"Who am I supposed to be fooling around with? Daphne?"

"She said you were taking her swimming in some natural pond tomorrow, in the nude." Rennie hissed, not wanting the others around the fire to hear.

"I never said that. I told her about the pond. If she wants to go swimming, that's her idea. It does get hot during the day and she complained about it all afternoon."

He paused a moment, then added, "Maybe swimming isn't a bad idea."

"In the nude?" Rennie exclaimed.

Amusement danced in Hunter's eyes as he watched her.

"What's the matter? Afraid I won't be able to resist her luscious charms if I see her unclothed?"

That was exactly what she was afraid of, but could she admit that to him?

"Men don't need love to *mate* with women," she threw out. "You told me that yourself."

His amusement vanished in an instant and a hard look came into his eyes. The soft, silvery glow turned into slate as his jaw tightened.

"You believe I'd sleep with her, don't you?"

"You sleep with me and you don't love me."

Please tell me I'm wrong, that you love me to distraction, her heart urged.

"I thought you were the woman who scorned love, didn't believe in it? Is that what you want now, protestations of undying love?"

His tone cut her to the quick.

She shook her head.

"Not if it isn't true," she said.

"I took those same vows you did, *Mrs. Bradshaw*, and I will adhere to them as you said you would. We're married, you and I, and that means I won't be sleeping with any other women."

His voice was hushed, but Rennie heard every word clearly.

"It isn't a normal marriage," she said.

"The hell it isn't."

"But we..."

"Maybe we didn't get married in the conventional manner, but it sure is going to be a normal marriage. So you put away any thoughts of sulking or pouting and make the most of it."

She nodded.

He didn't love her. She wasn't sure that anything was settled about Daphne, but she understood that he wanted to end the discussion. That much was clear.

"Tomorrow you ride with Jacko," he said, turning around and stomping back to the fire.

Jacko.

Another day apart from Hunter, while Daphne rode with him to the pond where they'd swim.

Her eyes stung with unshed tears and Rennie blinked rapidly to still them. She refused to weep in front of all these people, no matter how strong the provocation. She raised her head and marched to the stack of sleeping bags. Drawing hers, she went to bed down near the horse corral. Two of the drovers were stretched out near by, eyes already closed. The rest of the group sat around the fire, drinking coffee and talking.

Laughter rang out as Rennie spread her bag, but she ignored it, feeling lonely, lost and decidedly unloved.

She woke some time during the night. It was still and silent except for the muffled clomps from the horses in the makeshift corral. She snuggled down in her bag, warm and comfortable. Overhead the stars were brilliant in the dark, clear sky. They shimmered against the black velvet, the constellations strange to one raised in the northern hemisphere. She watched them for a few moments, knowing she'd never seen stars so radiant before.

Rolling on to her back, she banged into another body. Startled, she looked over. It was Hunter. He'd spread his sleeping-bag right next to hers. He appeared asleep, but then his arms came out and scooted her up against him, sleeping-bag and all.

"Go back to sleep," he murmured, his arm a familiar heavy weight across her ribs.

Rennie complied, oddly reassured by his presence.

He was gone when she arose the next morning and for a moment Rennie wondered if she'd imagined him during the night. But his sleeping bag was still there.

Ready to leave camp when Jacko was, she smiled at the young drover. It wasn't his fault that her husband had paired her with him. She and Jacko rode east then south, the first to leave.

Despite longing to be with Hunter, Rennie enjoyed the day. Her natural friendliness soon had Jacko explaining exactly what he did around the station.

He told her about the other drovers, where they were from, when they'd started work at Silver Creek Station, what their tasks were. He mentioned that his own family was from Queensland, and inquired about hers.

Rennie plied him with questions and knew she had a much better knowledge of the station after their day together.

Constantly in the back of her mind, however, Rennie saw Daphne and Hunter swimming in some secluded pond. *Skinny dipping.* She burned with jealousy. There was nothing she could do about it.

She'd made her feelings known to him last night and he'd ignored them. She wished Daphne would hurry up and go back to Sydney and never return.

But the latter was unlikely as she was Kerry's aunt.

Would her parents cause any trouble about the adoption? If they challenged Hunter's claim and won, then Kerry would go to live with the Adams. Would Hunter want a divorce then?

His primary reason for their marriage had been a mother for Kerry. If she was gone, there'd be no reason to remain married.

It was almost dusk by the time Jacko and Rennie rode into the camp. A quick glance around and Rennie knew that Hunter and Daphne hadn't yet come in.

Discouragement settled over her like a cloak. It might have been better to stay at the homestead. At least she could have imagined Hunter working with the stock men rather than pairing with Daphne.

George met her as she dismounted.

"Rennie, there's been an accident. Daphne injured her ankle and we had to call for medical aid. Ben flew down and picked up her and Hunter and took them back to the homestead."

"Hunter went back with her?" she asked in disbelief.

"Someone had to go with her. She's our guest. We couldn't very well send her back alone. Phil told me when I reached camp."

"How did it happen?" Rennie asked, trying to take in what George was saying.

She couldn't concentrate, could only think about Daphne and Hunter back at the homestead while she was over a hundred kilometers and several days" ride away to the south.

"Don't know. We have the small radios. Hunter called Phil who was packing the main radio. He found them, called for help and Ben was able to find a flat area not too far from where they were. Phil brought in their horses."

Rennie nodded. Now what? Daphne and Hunter alone for several days? What would that mean?

172 | BARBARA MCMAHON

"Are we going back now?" Rennie asked.

"No. We'll continue until tomorrow, the next day swing east, then after that head back."

"Will Hunter rejoin us?" she asked hopefully as they reached the fire and she gratefully accepted a plate of food.

"Not likely. It wasn't easy for Ben to land where he did. He doesn't want to take any unnecessary chances. We can manage. I ran this outfit until a couple of years ago. I haven't forgotten how."

She nodded, not caring at all about George's running things. What she wanted was to be with Hunter, and for Daphne to be in Sydney. Maybe she'd have left by the time they returned to the homestead?

Rennie sighed. She knew that that was highly unlikely. It looked as if she was settling in forever. How convenient to injure herself enough to require a return to the homestead, yet not to incapacitate herself entirely.

Rennie could do nothing to hurry the passing of the next four days, so she made the most of her situation. She took turns riding with each of the drovers, learning more about cattle than she'd ever thought possible, learning more about the men who worked Silver Creek Station.

She was the wife of the boss, and they treated her with respect and admiration. They were genuinely pleased with her interest and questions and set out to teach her all they knew.

It was a tired, dirty, bedraggled crew that rode into the main homestead late on the afternoon of the fifth day after Hunter and Daphne had flown home. The aching muscles of early in the trip had eased and Rennie was proud that she'd stayed the course.

She was anxious to see Hunter, almost fearful to learn if anything had changed because of their separation.

Kerry was playing outside with Maggie and heard the horses. She ran to greet them, excited to see her great-grandfather and Rennie. George dismounted and gave her a quick hug, then he lifted her up to Rennie.

"Give her a ride around the yard once, she'll love that."

Prattling a mile a minute, with only a word here and there that Rennie could understand, Kerry was in heaven riding.

Rennie had missed the toddler and hugged her gently to her as they circled the yard.

Where was Hunter? she wondered.

Dismounting after George took the baby, she was grateful when Jacko came for her horse.

"You go on in and get cleaned up. I'll see to the horse. Pleasure to have you with us on the drive," he said as he led the horse to the barn.

Rennie smiled tiredly and turned to fall in step with George.

"Where's Hunter?" she couldn't wait to ask.

"Maggie said he took Daphne into town. She had to see the doctor again about her ankle. Broke it, you know. They were putting on a walking cast today."

So she hadn't left.

Was she planning to move in with them Rennie wondered.

"Well, that will give us a chance to get cleaned up. I never realized how much I relished showers until we had to make do with washing out of a pan."

She grinned at Kerry, feeling as dirty as the baby sometimes got playing in the yard.

"Maggie has dinner started. I'll finish it. Give you a chance to rest up," George said.

"You were right there with me all the way. You must be tired, too."

"A bit, but I'm used to it. Won't be fancy tucker. Go on and get cleaned up."

Feeling a warm glow because of their new truce, Rennie hurried upstairs to shower and dress in clean clothes.

Had Hunter missed her while she'd been gone? She had sure missed him.

The Ute pulled into the yard as Rennie was dressing. She waited with baited breath for Hunter to come upstairs to see her. Slowly she dried her hair, put on a bit of make-up, surprised to see how tanned she'd become, despite wearing a hat every day. The blue of her eyes was brighter, the color in her cheeks becoming. She looked healthy and vibrant.

The minutes dragged by and Hunter didn't come. She heard the murmur of voices, then the men moved into the office.

Slowly Rennie stared at herself in the mirror, disappointment filling her. He wasn't hurrying up to see his wife. He'd see her in due time, at dinner.

She had her answer—he hadn't missed her.

When she was dressed, she started downstairs. She'd check on what Maggie had started for dinner, set the table, keep herself busy. She wouldn't seek Hunter out. He knew she was home. If he wanted to see her he'd find her.

As she was passing the phone in the hall, it rang. Picking it up automatically, she didn't even think of the one in the office. George could have answered.

"Hello?" she said.

"Rennie? It's Gerry Dalton, how are you?"

Gerry. And she'd never responded to his gift. She felt embarrassed.

"I'm fine, Gerry."

"I called a few days ago, but Maggie said you and Hunter were out on the station. Saw Hunter in town today so I knew you were back. Did you like the roses?"

"Oh, Gerry."

Damn, why hadn't Hunter handled this as he'd said he was going to? Now she was placed in a most awkward situation.

"Actually, I loved them. They were very pretty. But I couldn't keep them. I...we had this trip and I just got back today. And I wanted to finish decorating the house before starting the garden and all. I gave them back to Mamie Jordan. But they were beautiful and I thank you for thinking of me," she finished in a rush.

There was a moment of silence on the other end.

"I'm glad you liked them. I didn't consider that you might not be ready for them. No problem. I'm sure Mamie will let you have them when you're ready to plant. How did you like seeing a bit more of Silver Creek?"

"It was great. It's still hard to believe how big it is. And I learned so much about ranching on the outback."

Daphne opened the screen door and hobbled into the hall, her eyes on Rennie, a sly grin on her face.

Rennie was immediately conscious that the other woman would cause trouble because of the phone call if she knew it was Gerry on the other end.

"Yeah, when we were boys, Hunter and I would go out for weeks at a time. It was great. But cattle never interested me like they do Hunter."

"I have to go—dinner's cooking," she said gently, wanting to end the conversation before it went on too long.

"Sure thing. See you next time you're in town."

"Fine. Bye."

Hanging up gently, Rennie looked up at Daphne.

"How's your ankle?" she asked politely.

"Better. Who was your phone call to? Surely not Gerry Dalton?"

Rennie debated whether to answer or not, but before she decided the men came out of the office.

"Rennie, hi. Did you enjoy the trip?"

Hunter spotted her standing near the stairs, and strode over to her. When he saw Daphne's expression, his became wary. He made no move to kiss her.

"I enjoyed it," Rennie said shortly, acutely aware that she hadn't seen him in a number of days and all he'd done was ask after her trip.

No hug, no kiss, no mention of missing her.

She sighed softly. What had she expected? He'd been clear in telling her that he wasn't looking to fall in love.

"I can't believe it," Daphne said, her eyes on Rennie. "Gone for a week and when you get back you call Gerry Dalton before greeting your own husband?"

"I didn't call Gerry, he called here." She was tired of Daphne's constant trying to cause problems. The woman needed a life.

"How did he know you were home?" Hunter asked, his voice quiet.

"He saw you and Daphne in town today."

"So he couldn't wait to call you?"

"He wondered about the roses. I should have sent him a note or something. It was rude just to ignore him," she replied patiently.

"Rude be damned! I told you—"

"You told me you'd take care of the situation. When? After he's called here a dozen times? Don't get mad at me because he called. If you don't like it, you change it."

She stormed out to the kitchen and yanked the top off the simmering vegetables.

She jumped when she heard the office door slam shut. In only a moment George strolled in.

"He's taking care of the matter now," he said.

"Your grandson is enough to drive a person to...to..."

She was so angry she couldn't think of anything strong enough to reflect how she really felt. Blast it all, but he made her so mad!

George nodded, his expression thoughtful.

Hunter remained silent throughout dinner. Daphne sat with a self-satisfied smile on her face, her eyes darting between Hunter and Rennie. George and Rennie tried to keep the conversation going by discussing Kerry and reminiscing about the camping trip.

When he was finished, Hunter rose and excused himself.

"I'm going to talk to Jacko," he said, sweeping his gaze around the table.

Without another word, he left.

"I'll do the dishes tonight, Rennie. You spend some time with the baby," George said, rising.

She nodded, surprised at his offer. Hadn't he been the one a few days ago to comment that dishes were woman's work?

Grateful to have something to do, she picked up Kerry and carried her upstairs. With her foot in a cast, Daphne's mobility was limited, so Rennie didn't think she'd have to worry about her wanting to spend a lot of time with Kerry tonight.

With Hunter, maybe.

She enjoyed playing with the baby. When she noticed the additional toys in the room, she wondered how often Hunter and Daphne had gone into town.

But she was happy to see Kerry receive some attention from her aunt. Her arrival had not been auspicious.

Having kept the baby up as long as she dared, Rennie reluctantly left her room once she was asleep. Pausing at the top of the stairs, she wondered if she should just go into her own room and read before going to bed.

But she lifted her chin. She wouldn't be driven into retreat by Daphne. If she wanted to join them on the veranda, she had every right to do so. Maybe she'd find out how much longer Daphne planned to stay. It was well beyond the original five days now.

She walked firmly down the stairs, her sandals slapping against the wooden steps.

"Oh, Hunter!"

Daphne's exclamation was soft. So they were both on the veranda.

Taking a deep breath, Rennie pushed open the screen door and stopped in shock.

Daphne was sitting on Hunter's lap, her arms around his

neck, his hands resting at her side. For a long moment Rennie stared at the two of them, unable to believe her eyes, unable to believe the shaft of pain that pierced her at the sight.

It was Stuart all over again.

She was stunned. Her breath caught and for a moment she wondered if her heart would shatter. She couldn't believe it.

"Rennie."

Hunter shot up, steadying Daphne and reaching up to release her grasp, pulling her arms down to her side.

Even her business-arranged marriage was a mockery, Rennie thought. Hunter was like Stuart and every other man. All his fine words that night at the camp had been only that—words. Words that meant nothing.

She spun around, not knowing where to go to ease the pain. She couldn't believe it happened to her again.

"Rennie, wait."

He grabbed Daphne's arm and pulled her across the veranda until he reached Rennie. Grasping her arm in his free hand, he held on to both women, the planes and angles in his face hard in the light from the hall.

"Tell her, Daphne and tell her quick," Hunter said, his eyes never leaving Rennie's.

"What, darling?" Daphne cooed, her eyes also on Rennie, her smile daring.

Shaking her a little, Hunter turned on her.

"You little witch. Tell her what just happened or you can bloody well walk back to Sydney, starting right now!"

His voice was icy.

Daphne licked her lips and shrugged.

"I lost my balance. This cast is new. I'm not used to it," she said insolently, trying to release her arm from his hard grasp.

"I see," Rennie said, refusing to look at either one of them.

She knew better than to try to shrug off Hunter's grip.

"Dammit, Rennie, don't go seeing things that aren't there!" Hunter said.

Like love that wasn't there.

Like loyalty and steadfastness.

Like devotion from the man she loved.

No, she wouldn't see things that weren't there, no matter how much she wanted them.

"I won't," she said firmly. "I just came to tell you I was retiring early. I'm very tired from the drive and tonight's the first night in ages that I can sleep in a real bed. It sounds good."

Even to her own ears the words sounded hollow. But she pulled away from Hunter and turned to walk back up the stairs.

When would she learn?

Nothing had changed. And nothing would in the future. Was this the kind of life she wanted?

Slowly closing the door, Rennie leaned against it for a long moment, wondering. Was having Kerry enough? Was being only part of a family, not fully accepted, enough? Could she stay if there was love only on one side?

Rennie hoped that Hunter would follow her. Even his anger would give her some sign that she meant something to him.

But he didn't follow her and she knew he regarded the issue as closed. Sighing softly, she pushed away from the door and dressed for bed.

She awoke in the night, conscious of Hunter beside her. His hand held her possessively against his warm body. His breath fanned across her cheek, warm and soft as he breathed. Closing her eyes, Rennie imprinted in her mind the feel of every inch of him against her. She liked the weight of his arm across her. Liked the warmth from his legs as they lay tangled with hers.

Cherished the intimacy of sharing a bed in the dark. Her heart swelled with love. She wanted their marriage to work. What could she do to make sure it didn't end over Daphne? Would steadfastness on her part be enough? Would Hunter ever come to care for her?

Surely they'd started to build a foundation. It wouldn't be destroyed in one night. She'd give it a little longer. Maybe she'd see some sign in Hunter that would reassure her that they had a chance.

Hunter was long gone when she awoke the next morning. The bed was cold. Having dressed, she hurried downstairs to prepare breakfast, thinking back wistfully to the morning before their trip when he'd wakened her and kissed her.

"Looks like rain today," Hunter said as he came in from the yard just as she was dishing up pancakes.

He walked over to her and tilted her face to his gaze with one warm finger. Studying her for a moment, he seemed satisfied. Rennie's heart began beating rapidly. She gazed into his silvery eyes and longed to throw herself into his arms.

He dropped a brief kiss on her lips and went to sit at the

table. She touched her tongue to her lips, wishing the kiss had been longer, deeper. Blushing at her own thoughts, she hurried to serve breakfast.

George began eating, making no comments about Hunter's kiss. Rennie was grateful; she couldn't have stood being teased. She studied Hunter as she served his pancakes and made sure he could reach the butter and jam.

Why had he kissed her? He hadn't kissed her yesterday when she'd arrived home after several days" absence. He hadn't kissed her last night.

Now he was acting like an old married man giving his wife a good-morning greeting. She was confused.

"About time we had some rain," George said. "I'm always glad the first few storms. Then it gets old. But it's been months now since we've had any."

"Will this bring out the wildflowers?" Rennie asked as she began eating. She remembered what Hunter had told her about the flowers filling the fields after the rain and longed to see the transformation.

"Don't know how much water we'll get. The clouds are building. It could get bad. But usually we won't see many flowers after only one storm. I'm going out this morning, but will be back early. No need to get wet this early in the season. There'll be plenty of days later," Hunter said easily.

"Can I come with you?" Rennie asked.

"Not today. Stay in with Kerry. She missed you while you were gone."

She nodded, realizing that she hadn't really expected him to invite her to join him. But she wanted to do something to strengthen their tenuous ties.

"Take something up to Daphne, would you? It's hard for her to get around on that cast, and if she eats breakfast in bed she can take her time getting dressed," Hunter said as he prepared to leave.

Rennie nodded, her eyes on her plate. The last thing she wanted to do was play nursemaid to Daphne. But she'd be hospitable. The woman was their guest.

When Rennie took the breakfast tray to Daphne's room, the blond was already awake, but hadn't gotten up yet. She looked disappointed when Rennie opened her door.

"Thank you, Rennie. Hunter usually brings it to me, but I guess he turned over the chore to you now that you're home."

She smiled brightly, but Rennie didn't trust her one inch. Nor did she like the fact that Hunter had been coming into Daphne's bedroom every morning.

She'd make sure in the future that he needn't bother.

"I suppose. Do you need anything else?"

She longed to see Kerry and let their guest fend for herself.

"I'm sorry about last night. Hunter said I was naughty to tease you so. Truly, I tripped and fell into his lap. I was lucky he caught me," Daphne said, watching Rennie's reaction.

Rennie shrugged.

"I'm getting Kerry up now; holler if you want anything."

"Is Hunter around?"

"He's gone out."

"I guess after days of hanging around the house with me he needs to see to things outside now," Daphne murmured smugly, and began sipping her coffee.

Rennie refused to be drawn by the obvious taunt and

merely smiled and left to get Kerry up and dressed for the day.

By the time she had removed Daphne's tray and finished the dishes, however, she was seething. Daphne kept up a running commentary of what she'd done with Hunter, always insinuating the most intimate scenes.

Rennie didn't know whether to believe her or not, but the mere fact that she'd say such things was driving her crazy. She wanted to get away and find a breathing space.

When the phone rang, she hastened to answer it. George had been in the office earlier, but he'd left to work on some equipment.

"Rennie Bradshaw?"

"Yes."

"James Doolittle, at the post office in Boolong Creek. We have several large boxes for you. Just arrived this morning."

Rennie smiled. What a perfect opportunity to get out of the house for a while.

"Great! I'll come in today and pick them up."

"More than the normal mail here," he warned.

"I know; they're my things from America. I'll be in soon."

Hanging up, Rennie smiled. She had a legitimate excuse to go into town and escape Daphne for a few hours. And she couldn't wait to pick up the boxes. Maybe with some of her own things around she'd feel more like she belonged.

"Gerry Dalton's call, I assume, from your happy look?"

Daphne said as she hobbled into the hall from the living-room. She had a magazine dangling from one hand, and her rampant curiosity showed on her face. Had she been eavesdropping?

"Don't be silly," Rennie said impatiently. "But I do have

to go into town for a while. Can you watch Kerry?"

"Of course, I'm her aunt, aren't I?"

Rennie eyed her, not wanting to get into that discussion.

"I'll feed her lunch and put her down for her nap. Can you manage if she wakes up before anyone gets back?"

Rennie was already wondering how long it would take to drive in, load the boxes and drive back. Three hours should do it.

"Sure. I'm slow with this thing, but not totally immobile. What should I tell Hunter?" Daphne asked slyly.

Rennie's hackles rose and she frowned, then tossed her head.

"I'll deal with Hunter. You needn't worry about it."

11

It was only when Rennie started out for Boolong Creek that she remembered Hunter's saying it was going to rain. From the look of the dark clouds to the north, it would be a fierce storm when it hit. But the sun still shone on the homestead. Maybe the rain would hold off for a few more hours.

By the time she pulled out on to the blacktop and glanced at the horizon, she could see rain in the distance. She hesitated a moment, then accelerated. She wanted to go to town, needed to escape Daphne's company. And she'd been driving in rain all her life–how bad could the storm be?

Reaching the outskirts of Boolong Creek, Rennie had an indication of how bad the storm could be. The rain had started and was torrential, pouring down so hard and fast that her wiper blades were ineffective. Commencing about ten minutes from town, it had been like driving beneath a powerful fire hose. Already she could see puddles forming beside the road as the parched ground was unable to soak up the water fast enough.

The shallow culvert beneath the wooden bridge near Boolong was running muddy water. Sheets of rain extended as far as Rennie could see. She was enveloped by the storm.

She only hoped the post office would have a sheltered entrance so that her boxes didn't get soaked being loaded into the Land Rover. Though if the winds that buffeted her car were as strong in town she didn't have a chance of keeping them from getting wet.

Nothing short of driving into the building would keep her dry, she realized a short time later as she and one of the men from the post office loaded the boxes into her car. The slight overhang was mostly for show, and the heavy rain and gusting wind soon soaked through the light jacket that she'd found in the car. Her hair was wet, even her jeans were saturated. But she finished loading the boxes, filling the back of the large vehicle.

These were the boxes of her things. She'd sold all but a few items when she'd left Texas. This, combined with what she'd flown to Australia with, represented everything she owned in the world.

She'd have to call Gram tonight and let her know that everything had arrived, check to see how she was doing. Emails weren't the same as talking with someone. Maybe she could even talk to her about Hunter.

Thanking the man for his help, she climbed into the car and turned the heat up to high. Shivering slightly, she maneuvered the vehicle around and headed for home. She'd have liked to dry out a little at Mattie's, have a cup of hot tea or something, but the weather was so bad that she wanted to get home as soon as she could.

It appeared almost dark although it was the middle of the afternoon. She held the car on the road with effort as the wind whipped across her path, buffeting the sturdy Land Rover. Slowly she drove through town and turned on to the road that led to Silver Creek Station. Maybe she'd see the Silver Creek after all this rain.

Maybe. But right now all she saw was Boolong Creek. It had grown to a river, wide and muddy and swirling across the small bridge that normally spanned the dry creek bed. Rennie pulled the car to a stop at the water's edge and peered through the blurry windshield in dismay. She'd have to ford it to get to the other side, and she didn't know how deep it was. Nor where the sides of the bridge actually ended. Was it slightly wider than the blacktop? If she drove down the middle would she be all right?

She was afraid. Glancing to her left at the roiling water, she wondered if she should try. She'd heard tales of flash-floods was this one? Would she get halfway across and be inundated by a wall of water? Swept away?

Just then she saw flashing lights in her mirror. Turning, she watched as Gerry Dalton's official car draw to a halt behind her. In seconds he was at her window, wearing a yellow slicker streaming with water.

Rolling down the window, she felt the pelting rain. He at least had a proper slicker.

"Rennie, what are you doing here?"

Gerry was clearly startled to see her. He tried to block the rain as he leaned over the window.

"I was trying to go home but I'm afraid to cross this river."

She gestured toward the torrent before them.

"I came down to check on it. It has a tendency to flood in weather like this. I don't recommend your trying it. The current can be excessively strong when its this high. It'll subside soon after the rain stops. Shouldn't be more than a couple of hours."

"A couple of hours?"

She looked at the creek, wondering once again if she should try it. Had it risen even as they'd been talking?

"Head back to town. When it subsides you can go home. Call the folks if you think they'll worry."

She nodded reluctantly. Gerry's advice was good. She really didn't want to risk it. She'd have something hot to drink at Mattie's and wait out the storm.

Rennie sat sipping her tea a few minutes later. She'd dried her hair as best she could in the ladies" room, taken her damp jacket off and slung it across the back of her chair. Mattie had a small heater working in the rear and Rennie sat as close to its warmth as she could, conscious of her damp shoulders and jeans.

The tea was good, as was the berry pie she'd just finished. Outside she could still see the rain splashing in the street, the dark sky, hear the wind.

She sat at the same table that she and Hunter had shared on her first day. As she drank, she remembered their conversation. So much had happened in a few weeks. But her attraction to the man hadn't diminished a bit. She wished he were here. She wouldn't worry about the drive home if he were behind the wheel.

She'd put off calling the homestead in hopes the rain would ease up and she could cross the bridge. But it didn't look as if it was abating. She shivered, still cold.

What if the storm continued all night? Good grief, what a mess. She should have waited to come in but she'd been so impatient to get away from Daphne's innuendos that she'd jumped at the opportunity to come to town.

And she'd never expected the storm to be this bad.

Gerry Dalton opened the door and entered, cool air rushing in with him. Glancing around the nearly deserted cafe, he spotted Rennie immediately and headed her way. Shedding his slicker, he hung it over a nearby chair and pulled out the one opposite her.

"You call home?" he asked as he sat down.

"Not yet. I was hoping it'd stop."

He shook his head. "Not likely for a while. There's a call box just outside. Take my slicker and keep dry," he offered.

She slipped it on. It was way too big, but at least it'd keep the rain off. Going out into the storm, Rennie was surprised at how cool the afternoon had grown. At least Mattie's was warm and dry.

She fed the machine and soon heard the ring at the other end. The line was full of static and she held the receiver away from her ear just a little.

"Hello?" George answered.

"Grandpa? This is Rennie."

"Where the hell are you, girl? It's raining cats and dogs."

"I know. I'm in Boolong Creek, at Mattie's."

The static was awful. She held the receiver further away while she spoke.

"Gerry closed the bridge."

"I can't hear you, Rennie. Speak up."

His voice was faint.

Raising her voice, she continued, "I'm not coming home..."

There was a large shriek in the phone line.

She shook her head, and tried again. "I'm not coming home until the rain lets up. But I'm fine."

There was nothing but static on the line.

"Grandpa?"

Nothing.

Slowly Rennie hung up. She hoped he'd heard her and they wouldn't worry about her at the homestead.

She looked up the street. The rain was still thundering down, the water sheeting across the blacktop, puddling here and there. Shivering, Rennie hurried back to the warmth of Mattie's.

"Thanks, Gerry," she said as she shed the dripping slicker.

"Get through all right?"

"I think so. There was a lot of static, and then the line went dead, but I told George I was here."

As she resumed her seat, she noticed that he'd ordered a cup of hot coffee. Sitting across from him, she suddenly realized how awkward she felt, knowing that Hunter had told her to stay away from him.

Exactly what had Hunter told Gerry on the phone?

"I'd invite you to my place to wait out the storm, but Hunter would have my head. He's pretty possessive," Gerry said. He tilted his head and asked quizzically, "Did I overstep the bounds somewhere, Rennie? I didn't mean to."

She shook her head.

"No. I know Hunter was upset about the roses, but..."

She didn't know what to say.

"But he's possessive. Yeah, I know. He made that real clear when he called. Stay away from his wife."

Finishing up his coffee, he rose.

"Duty calls. I'll let you know when the water's down enough for you to go home."

She smiled her thanks and watched him leave. Now what? She had who knew how long to wait. Leaning back in the chair, she wished she had a book to read, or some stationery, so that she could write her friends in Texas and tell them all about life on the outback.

Rennie was on her third pot of tea and just finishing her second letter on a tablet that one of the waitresses had found in the back when Gerry returned. He nodded to some of the patrons who had sought to get out of the storm at Mattie's, then headed back toward Rennie's table.

"Still raining, I see," she said.

She smiled at the water that streamed off his slicker.

"Yes, but easing some. I checked the bridge—still covered, but once the rain stops the water level should drop enough for you to cross an hour or so later. I'll go with you in case you get into any trouble."

"I appreciate that."

Especially if the water still covered the bridge.

Gerry ordered another cup of coffee and sat with Rennie while the waitress poured it.

"Any accidents?" she asked.

"None. Most people stayed inside when they saw how bad it was going to be."

"Like I should have," Rennie said wryly.

Gerry nodded. "But you didn't know it would be this bad."

"No. In fact, it didn't even start raining until I was almost in town. Then it came so fast and so hard, I could hardly see to drive."

"Not our usual weather, but not uncommon either."

At that moment the door to Mattie's slammed open and Hunter Bradshaw strode into the room. He wore a fleece-lined denim jacket, already damp on the shoulders, skin-tight jeans and muddy boots. His hat was dark with rain. He paused for only a moment before his eyes lit on Rennie. As he strode over to the table, his boots sounded abnormally loud in the quiet room.

All conversation stopped and all eyes watched him.

In his hand was a large bouquet of red roses, water dripping from the open blossoms. His eyes narrowed when he saw Gerry stand and turn to face him, then he looked beyond Gerry and caught Rennie's eye.

Never moving his gaze, he stormed over to the table and laid the wet flowers down on the table. He looked taller than normal and angry.

Rennie felt the spray from the roses splatter her shirt. The water was cold. She looked up at Hunter. He was furiously angry. She sighed. What next?

He turned to Gerry, his eyes cold as slate.

"What the hell are you doing with my wife?"

Rennie had never heard such anger in her life. She was mesmerized by the scene before her. She should explain, but she didn't know exactly why Hunter was so mad. Just because Gerry was with her? She hardly knew the man and for heaven's sake, they were in a public restaurant.

Before she could say anything, however, Gerry spoke.

"Discussing when the bridge might be passable. Guess you came over it?"

After a flickering glance at the table, Hunter faced Gerry again, his stance menacing, his hands balled into fists.

"It took you a cup of coffee to explain about the bridge? I could have done it in three seconds."

Rennie looked down at the roses lying in splendor before her. Their fragrance filled the air, the drops of water like crystal on the velvety petals. Where had he gotten roses?

There was something significant in the flowers, and she stopped listening to the men as she tried to figure out what it was.

There were no roses on Silver Creek Station. So where had Hunter gotten these? Mamie Jordan was the only one Rennie knew who grew roses. Had Hunter gone there and cut this bouquet? In the pouring rain?

Vibrant, deep scarlet roses. Velvet petals and a fragrance to fill the room.

Red roses meant love. Did Hunter know that?

She raised her head and stared at him. He looked as if he was about to hit Gerry.

"Hunter," she said softly, her eyes soft with wonder and hope and love.

He glared at her.

"I'll deal with you when I'm finished with him," he snapped.

Rennie rose and drew on the light jacket. She picked up her letters and stuffed them into her bag. Taking the bouquet, she cradled it in her arms and moved around the table to step between Hunter and Gerry. The air shimmered with tension. But she refused to have these two men, one-time friends, coming to blows because of her.

Reaching up, she placed her warm palm against Hunter's cool cheek. His startled gaze dropped to hers.

"Thank you for coming for me. I thought I'd be here for hours."

"You couldn't get away?"

His hand covered hers, pulling it down from his face. But his fingers tightened around hers and didn't release her. He frowned at Gerry.

"Sorry if the rain ruined your plans. You'll find I don't give up my wife as easily as Alex did."

"What the hell are you talking about?" Gerry asked, puzzled.

"Grandpa said Rennie called to say she wasn't coming back. But she is. Even if I had to follow you two to Darwin, Sydney or even Texas. She's my wife."

His hand tightened against Rennie's. But she didn't notice the ache.

She only heard his declaration that he would have followed her all the way to Texas if she'd gone there. Her heart was pounding heavily in her chest, hope soared within her.

Surely he wouldn't say such a thing if he didn't care for her?

She took a breath, the fragrant scent of the flowers overwhelming her senses. The tight hold on her hand burned itself into her mind. He held what was his.

"The line went dead," she said.

"What?"

He looked at her.

"The line went dead when I was talking to Grandpa. I said I wouldn't be home until the worst was over and the bridge was open."

"What the hell are you doing here in town anyway?"

196 | B<small>ARBARA</small> M<small>C</small>M<small>AHON</small>

"I came for the rest of my things. My boxes arrived today from Texas and I came to get them. I didn't know the storm would be so bad. Even in Texas we rarely get storms this bad."

"You weren't running off with Gerry?"

She heard Gerry's muttered expletive behind her, but never looked away from the dear face of the man she loved.

"Why would I ever want to run off with Gerry? My family is at Silver Creek Station," she replied softly.

My love is there.

"Just for the record, Hunter, I don't run off with other men's wives," Gerry said, his voice loud in the silent cafe.

Hunter met his eyes and for a long moment neither spoke.

"What about Tessa?" Hunter asked at last.

"What about her?" Gerry looked startled. "You think I ran off with her? Good God! I was headed to Darwin that day she called and asked for a lift. I didn't know until later that she was leaving Silver Creek Station. All this time you thought I was running off with her?"

Hunter nodded.

Gerry snagged his slicker and put it on. He adjusted the hat and glanced first at Rennie, then Hunter.

"There's no reaching you if you believed that about me after twenty-five years of knowing me."

With that, Gerry turned and left the cafe.

Rennie's fingers were numb. Gingerly she tried pulling her hand free as Hunter watched Gerry leave.

He swept his eyes around the room and heads swiveled away from him. Conversations began again. Soon Hunter and Rennie were ignored. A silent island of two in the cafe.

"Hunter, can we go now?"

He nodded, noticing her attempt to free her hand. Slowly his fingers relaxed, threaded through hers and he led the way from Mattie's out into the pouring rain. Rennie shivered from the sudden drop in temperature. The rain was not as fierce now, and the wind had died down. Maybe it'd stop altogether soon and she could make it across the bridge.

"The Land Rover is over there."

She pointed to it and Hunter nodded.

"You're coming with me. I'll send someone in later to get it."

In only moments they were safely ensconced in the big utility truck, the heater going full blast as Hunter drove out of town. He didn't pause at the water-covered bridge, but drove slowly across it, the water covering the tires. With no trouble he picked up speed and headed for Silver Creek Station.

"I can't believe you were with Gerry," he growled.

"A cup of coffee doesn't begin to compare with five days together, *Hunter, darling*," she returned, still dazed by the roses. How unlike Hunter to bring her flowers. He'd even stated once that he'd never do so.

Rennie didn't know what was going through his mind, but she sat quietly beside him, delighting in the beautiful flowers. They had dried in the warmth of the truck and their fragrance filled the cab.

Red roses meant love. Why had he brought them to her?

"Would you really have come all the way to Texas to get me?" she asked.

"I said so, didn't I?" he bit out.

"Why would you think I'd left in the first place?" she asked, astonished that he'd ever think such a thing.

Her love for him had not gone unnoticed by George. Had Hunter really no inkling of how she felt about him?

"Daphne told me you'd gone off with Gerry in response to some phone call this morning."

Rennie felt guilty for a moment. She hadn't denied Daphne's guess when she'd come out into the hall. Then reason reasserted itself.

"Do you ever feel that Daphne delights in causing trouble?" Rennie mused, thinking back to all the pain and anguish the woman had caused her with her insinuations and sly comments. The endless jealousy she'd felt.

"Sure, that's her stock-in trade. I've known that all along. The key is not to let her get to you."

"Easier said than done," Rennie murmured.

"If she thinks she can get to you, she'll keep it up. Once she knows she can't, she'll get bored and stop. What was she doing to upset you?"

Rennie looked over at him. His voice had been casual, but she wondered if there was more to it than mere curiosity. Wondered if she dared tell him. Searching her memory, she tried to find something that would give her a clue that Hunter might feel differently about their marriage than he'd said. That he might want more than the business arrangement they'd agreed to.

"Daphne knows ours is not a real marriage and constantly made sly comments about it. I guess she shook my confidence that we could make a go of it," she said sadly.

"We've been over this before, Rennie. Ours is a real marriage. The circumstances leading up to it weren't normal, maybe, but, make no mistake, this is what marriage is about.

You pull your weight at the homestead, I pull mine. Together we're building a life, raising Kerry. What's unreal about any of it?"

She was silent for a long time, not knowing how to explain herself without giving away the fact that she loved him almost desperately.

"Well?" he prompted.

"Well, I guess I thought there'd be something more. Something that would make it seem real."

"Such as?"

"Talking together. Like we did when I first came. Sharing ideas and dreams. Things like that."

She trailed of. She wasn't sure that was the only thing missing. But she'd enjoyed the first week when he'd taken her for walks around the homestead after dinner, just the two of them.

"I'm not much on talking, Rennie," he said heavily. "And I'm not much on being married, beyond what we have. Tessa and Alex's marriage is the only one I've really seen and they fought all the time. She was unhappy at the station and he couldn't live in the city. I thought we'd suit since you were from the country, were used to cattle, didn't want fancy clothes and trips to the city."

"We do suit," she said.

The last thing she wanted was for him to think she was unhappy the way Tessa had been.

"But you were so distant on the camping trip," she said.

"I was working. It wasn't an amusing outing for fun. It was work. Besides, I used that trip to help you. I paired you up with Grandpa thinking you two could get to know each other better. He shocked me when he sided with you at dinner that night though I had always hoped he'd eventually come around."

"And you paired me with Jacko. Why did I have to go with him?"

He smiled. "Wanted to be with me, eh?"

At her nod, his eyes lightened.

"Jacko could tell you all about the station, give you more insight into how things ran from his perspective. And it gave him a chance to know you. Grandpa said you rotated with all the men. Now you know them and that should strengthen your feelings of belonging."

She was silent. It was true. She did feel more a part of the station because of the trip.

Hunter had known that, had planned for that.

Seeing it in that light, she began to feel a warm glow.

"We've begun to forge bonds that will last a lifetime. We're married. We're adopting Kerry. We're good together in bed."

Rennie felt the familiar heat sweep through her. They were good together, all the time.

She loved him so much.

"What more could you want, sweetheart?" he asked as he kept his eyes on the rainy road. Shyly she placed her hand on his hard thigh. She could feel the tension in him and wondered at it. Was he still angry?

"Maybe love?"

"If what you want is love, I have a heart full for you, sweetheart," he said simply.

12

Rennie stared at him, noting the tension around his lips, the stiffness in his body. Almost as if he was prepared for a blow. As if he was afraid. Of what? She couldn't imagine this strong, arrogant rancher afraid of anything on earth.

Unless it was fear of her reaction to his words.

Was the mighty, arrogant, self-assured, macho, brash cowboy vulnerable to her reaction to his offer of love?

Her heart melted. Slowly the smile spread across her face as the gladness swept through her heart.

He loved her!

"Oh, Hunter!"

She flung herself against him in astonished delight.

The truck swerved and then steadied. Slowly Hunter drew it to a stop, pulling to the edge of the road. Leaving on the lights, he turned off the engine and turned to look at her in the waning afternoon light, his strong arms catching her against him, pulling her against the strength of his chest.

Rennie was surrounded by love, the heat within her rising up to meet the heat in his kiss.

His lips were hot and demanding and she met him every step of the way. The roses were forgotten as they dropped to the floor. She could only think of Hunter, only feel Hunter's love warming her for all time. Struggling to get closer, she felt the iron band of his arms hold her, never to let her go.

He loved her!

Rennie squirmed at the heat and desire that flooded her, and her elbow hit the horn, startling her.

"Damn, sweetheart, don't announce to the world what we're doing," Hunter murmured against her throat, his hands busy igniting every nerve-ending in her body.

"Traffic is non-existent," she whispered. "Oh, Hunter, I love you so much. I can't believe you love me! I've wanted you to so much, but you never seemed to be any different than that first day."

"Probably because I fell in love that first day. You knocked me for a loop when you climbed out of Ben's plane."

Hot, moist kisses stoked the flame within her and she gasped with the sensual shock that gripped her. Clasping his head to her, her fingers delighted in the texture of his thick hair, the strength of his muscular shoulders.

"I think I fell in love then, too," she said between kisses. "But I really knew I loved you when Daphne arrived. I've been so jealous of her. But I was afraid I was like my mother. I had thought I loved Stuart, only what I feel for you is so much stronger, different somehow, lasting. I could never love another man like I love you!"

"Glad to hear that, sweetheart. I wasn't sure of my own feelings at first, either. Whenever we seemed to draw closer you pulled back. I was afraid to push the issue."

"Because I thought you didn't believe in love. You said it often enough. Why didn't you tell me?"

"I didn't know when it hit me. But the thought of you with Gerry made me as jealous as Daphne did you. I was afraid you'd run off with him."

He hugged her tightly against him, his hand rubbing across her slender back.

"As to not telling you, I was looking for something that might indicate you were interested. Are you getting cold?"

She shook her head. "Never when I'm with you."

Feeling particularly bold, she kissed him. Her heart was ready to explode with happiness. How could a body contain it all?

"I like the feel of you, sweetheart," he said his silvery eyes gazing lovingly down into hers. "From the first moment, my body was drawn to yours. You were not at all what I expected from Aunt Marjorie's descriptions and I wanted you from the first."

"Me too. And I thought it was only on my side. You hid it well."

"Who's talking, Miss Snooty-wait-a-while-longer? I thought you'd come to my room that first time to make love and all you wanted was the car keys. I had a hard time falling to sleep that night."

"We'll never get home at this rate," she said, already feeling the magnetic pull of attraction between them, relishing the waves of pleasure that his hands generated. "You were right when you said we'd make love whenever you said. But I never would have suspected a truck."

He chuckled and put her firmly next to him, starting the engine. "A Ute has many uses, but as a bed it leaves a lot to be desired."

Once they were underway, he linked her hand in his and rested them on his thigh.

"About Daphne..." Rennie started again, still bemused by his declaration.

"We'll send her home tomorrow. I don't know when she'll be back, but she will come to visit from time to time. She's Kerry's aunt and I want Kerry to know her entire family."

"I know."

She sighed. She'd be tied to Daphne forever. But Kerry was worth it.

And henceforth Rennie knew she could face Daphne more courageously, confident in Hunter's love. She smiled with giddy glee. He loved her!

"When Kerry's older, she can visit her grandparents and aunt in Sydney."

"Daphne mentioned something like that."

"Once the adoption is final and we don't have to worry about custody battles, then we can let her visit. But she'll always be our little girl."

"She's another one I fell in love with at first sight," Rennie murmured, her thigh pressing against his.

The overwhelming awareness she always felt around him was as strong as ever. She smiled in delirious excitement–the attraction was mutual.

Reaching down to rescue her flowers from the floor, Rennie was pleased to see that they hadn't been damaged by the fall. She couldn't wait to put them in water.

"I can't believe you brought me roses. You must have cut them in the pouring rain."

"Mmm."

"Why?"

She couldn't envision him standing in the pouring rain choosing flowers for her. It didn't fit her image of the rough Aussie she'd married. The one who'd scorned romance.

Yet the proof lay in her lap.

He was silent for a long moment, then shrugged.

"You might as well know. I was furious when I got home and Daphne said you'd gone into town to see Gerry. You know how I felt about him. Then, before I could leave to come get you, Grandpa said you'd called and told him you weren't coming back. He heard something about Gerry as well."

"He hadn't heard what I really said because the connection was so bad. Gerry closed the bridge."

"Right. But I didn't know that then. I was mad as hell."

She shivered, knowing how he got when angry.

"But Grandpa stopped me before I left. He said women like romance, needed it, and asked where was the romance in our relationship. Even a relative stranger like Gerry had brought you flowers."

"And because of that you stopped for flowers?"

"I thought about what he said on the ride into town. Once I got some of the anger worked out, I thought about your not having any romance. You arrived and were immediately plunged into the household. You've mentioned we don't have any privacy. It was the same complaint Tessa had made. I remembered how happy you'd looked when you first saw the rose bushes. So I thought it'd make it easier to drag you home if I had some."

"So you were going to drag me home," she said wryly, amused now that she knew he loved her.

"Damn right. You're my wife!"

"Did you know that red roses mean love?" she asked, curious.

"Of course. Roses for my love. And mine had better be the only ones you get in the future. I'll buy you a dozen rose bushes and you can have roses every day of your life, if you want."

"Mostly I want you every day of my life," she said, snuggling closer, happiness threatening to burst her wide open.

"That you have, my only love, that you have."

"You might have mentioned it earlier," she said, thinking of the anguish of the last few weeks.

"But you were the one who scoffed at love."

"You did, too."

"Indeed, but in my case I had never seen it before. Didn't know what it felt like. But when I thought of you with Gerry I wanted to kill him and lock you in a room where no man could ever see you again."

"How primitive."

"That's how I feel around you."

"And here I thought you only wanted to mate with me because of some animal drive for propagation," she teased.

He chuckled, his hand tightening around hers.

"You were certainly innocent if you bought that one, sweetheart. I couldn't keep my hands off you. I'd never felt that way about any other woman before, not even Gina. I wanted to take you to bed on our wedding night. I thought I behaved admirably, holding off until my birthday."

"We fit together perfectly. I'll make you a good wife," she said earnestly.

"I know you will, you already have. Now do you think one day you could consider this a normal marriage? I want to start a family with you, sweetheart. Will you have my babies?"

She smiled and nodded.

"Of course."

What a wonderful father he'd make. He was already a fantastic husband. How much more would their love develop now that they both realized the love they shared?

For a fleeting moment she gave a thought to her mother and Tessa and even Hunter's mother. She wouldn't repeat their follies. She'd hold on to her love and her husband forever, reveling in the strength of their love and commitment to each other.

"I'd like to have roses near the veranda," she said wistfully as she stroked the velvety softness of the flowers in her lap.

"I'll buy you a dozen bushes and you will know every time you look at them, every time you pick a bouquet for the house, how much I love you."

She smiled in deep satisfaction as they rode through the rainy afternoon. She'd have to call Gram. Who would ever have suspected that Marjorie's legacy would bring so much happiness? With a silent thank-you to the old woman who had made it all possible, Rennie snuggled up to her husband and gazed out the rain-drenched windshield.

It was a glorious day.

Epilogue

R ennie opened the email and began to type.

Dear Gram,

    At last I'm sending the promised photographs. The first one is of Hunter. Isn't he gorgeous? I'm so happy, Gram. I didn't believe in love after Stuart but Hunter proved me wrong. I hadn't a clue how perfect life could be until now. I love him so much I almost ache and he loves me as much. I know I'll be happy right here for the rest of my life. We talked about getting a house of our own, but have decided to remain with Grandpa, though Hunter has forbidden him to come to the kitchen after dinner. Sorry, that's a private joke.

    The next photo is of our daughter, Kerry. Isn't she precious? The adoption is going fine and she'll be truly ours in only a few more weeks. She's talking up a storm now and into everything, but I wouldn't change a single thing about her. I only hope our own children are as delightful.

    Yes, there will be another generation for you to love and fuss over before much longer. Please get well enough to come here for the happy event. It will be in the spring, a pretty time to visit the outback. Hunter's talking about a boy. I told him I can make no promises, but he said it didn't matter.

    The next photo is of the horse Hunter bought me, with

the house in the background. The last is of Grandpa. I think he's starting to believe I mean to stay. He's happy for Hunter's happiness, and that's gone a long way to make him accept me. Who knows, in another few years I might even have enough of an Australian accent that he'll stop calling me "that Yank Hunter married."

I miss you, Gram. But, aside from the distance that separates us, I wouldn't change anything in my life. Now that I know Hunter loves me, I can face anything. Even Daphne. That's another family joke.

I'm so pleased everything is going well at your end and hope your recovery continues at such a rapid pace. Can't wait for you to see everything here and meet Hunter. You'll love him, if for no other reason than I do.

All my love, Rennie.

She attached the final photo and hit send.

If you liked **Wanted: Outback Wife**,
you'll enjoy book 1 in the Golden Gate Romance Series,
Billionaire's Betrothal.

If you enjoyed **Wanted: Outback Wife**,
please consider leaving a review.

More books by Barbara McMahon

Golden Gate Romance Series
Billionaire's Betrothal

Cowboys of Wildcat Creek
Valentine's Cowboy Rescue
Shelly and the Cowboy
Kristi's Cowboy Hero
Holly's Reluctant Cowboy
A Cowboy for Eliza

Sweet Reunion Romance Collection
Unexpected Reunion
Unpredictable Reunion
Unanticipated Reunion

The Talmadge Sisters
Letters to Caroline
Michelle's Marriage Deal
Trusting Abby

The Harts of Texas Series
Rebel Heart
Tangled Hearts
Reckless Heart

Cowboy Heroes Series
Blue Bells on the Hill
Cowboy's Bride
One Stubborn Cowboy
Crazy About a Cowboy
Never Doubt a Cowboy
Cowboy Marshal
Summer Cowboy
Second Chance Cowboy
Movie Star Cowboy

www.ingramcontent.com/pod-product-compliance
Lightning Source LLC
Chambersburg PA
CBHW061134200626
46817CB00016B/1397